The detective and gave her he got to his now, Dr Truscott. I think starting to get the picture. Thank you for your time.'

Keiva stared at him, her mouth dropping open in shock. 'You surely don't think I'm in some way responsible for those deaths?'

Liam gave her an inscrutable look. 'I make it a policy never to make assessments until all the evidence is before me. But I would appreciate it if you'd co-operate by staying in town until I've finished my enquiries.'

'You're barking up the wrong tree, Detective.' She threw him a resentful look. 'It's my job to save lives, not destroy them.'

Liam's grey-blue eyes hardened a fraction. 'It's my job to find out the truth, Dr Truscott, and I don't intend to leave Karracullen until I do.'

24:7

**The cutting edge of
Mills & Boon® Medical Romance™**

LIVING FOR THE MOMENT

The emotion is deep
The drama is real
The intensity is fierce

24:7

**Feel the heat—
every hour...every minute...every heartbeat**

HER PROTECTOR
IN ER

BY
MELANIE MILBURNE

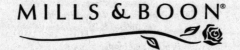

MILLS & BOON®

To my father, Gordon Luke, who was my very first hero. Love you, Dad.

Every day in my home state of Tasmania, and across the country of Australia, the dedicated men and women of the police force are here to protect and guide the population. I have had the privilege to work closely with some of these wonderful people as I researched this novel. My very heartfelt thanks go to: Inspector Ron Martin (Forensics—now retired), Inspector John Bird (Forensics) and Catherine Campbell (Toxicologist). I would also like to thank First Class Constable Steven Fry and Constable Joanne Fordham for their invaluable input in what it is to be a police officer in both the country and the city.
Thanks to all of you!

*First published in Great Britain 2005
Harlequin Mills & Boon Limited,
Eton House, 18-24 Paradise Road, Richmond, Surrey TW9 1SR*

© Melanie Milburne 2005

ISBN 0 263 84331 9

*Set in Times Roman 10 on 11¼ pt.
03-0905-54573*

*Printed and bound in Spain
by Litografia Rosés, S.A., Barcelona*

CHAPTER ONE

'LISTEN, Dr Truscott.' Barry Conning slapped the folder he was carrying onto the desk. 'This is the fifth unexpected death we've had in as many months. What the hell is going on?'

Keiva Truscott met the older man's frowning expression with a cool, composed stare. 'What exactly are you implying, Barry? That we're not running Accident and Emergency competently?'

Barry ran a hand through his thinning hair. 'Look, I know how hard you all work, you especially, but even you have to admit this is highly unusual. Karracullen is a country town. People come to this hospital for medical help, they don't expect to walk through those doors and a few days later be wheeled out in the back of a mortician's van. Our job is to save their lives, not send them on their way with wreaths around their necks.'

Keiva drew in a calming breath as she faced the medical superintendent. 'As far as I've been able to tell, all the patients you're referring to had myocardial infarctions and subsequently died. I'm sure you've reviewed the notes yourself, it's all documented there. I've personally reviewed these cases ten times each. People do still die of heart attacks you know.'

'I know that, but not one of these patients came in with heart problems.'

Keiva clicked the end of her pen once or twice, the breath she'd been holding whooshing out in resignation. 'Look, I'll go back through the notes again, see if there's anything I've missed, but I don't think it will achieve anything. I'm confident we did everything we could in each and every case. The human body is not like a machine where you can predict precise outcomes. It has a habit of doing its own thing at times, including having unexpected heart attacks. Disease can trigger all sorts of responses, heart attacks being one of them.'

'I hope you can quash any doubts in all these cases,' Barry said, loosening his tie as if he was suddenly finding it uncomfortable, 'because there's a detective arriving in a few minutes to interview you.'

Keiva straightened in her seat. 'A detective? What do you mean, a detective? Since when did this suddenly become a criminal investigation? We've presented all these cases at hospital Grand Rounds. It's a bad run, yes, but there's been no incompetent treatment. They've all been subjected to peer review, Barry!'

'Calm down, Keiva, will you? This hasn't come from within the hospital. You know this is a small town. There have been rumours, lots of them, and now complaints.' He took out his handkerchief and wiped his forehead. 'The Medical Registration Board has had five complaints in five months. They've approached Police Forensics for advice, and Forensics see a pattern, hence the detective making enquiries. He's interviewing everyone who's been working in A and E for the last year. You're first on his list.'

The pen she'd been holding rolled off the desk to the floor, but she didn't bother retrieving it.

'This is unbelievable! Why me first?'

Barry gave a shrug of one shoulder. 'You're the one who attended each patient.'

'I'm a doctor, for God's sake!' She sprang to her feet in agitation. 'It's my job to attend to patients. I run the A and E department.'

'You ordered the drugs and procedures,' Barry pointed out. 'He'll want to know what quantities and so on, go through your notes with you, that sort of thing.'

Keiva knew exactly what 'that sort of thing' meant. She had little time for the police after what had happened to her father. Their heavy-handed and guilty-until-proven-innocent approach had done more damage than she wanted to think about. It had been ten years and still the sound of a siren made her blood boil.

'Well, I don't finish until nine this evening,' she said. 'He'll have to wait, unless you want me to close A and E.'

'No, of course not, but let's hope he's a patient man,' Barry answered, and shouldered open the door to leave.

Keiva sat down as soon as the door swung shut behind him, her eyes coming to rest on the folder in front of her.

Five people had died soon after they had been in her care. No doctor liked those sort of statistics on their record but she'd done all she could. She was confident she'd followed the appropriate procedure in each case. She could even recall faces and figures. Patients had never been nameless numbers to her; she could recall each and every one as if she'd treated them yesterday.

Pat Grafton had come in with renal colic, not heart symptoms, although he had been overweight and slightly breathless. She'd administered pethidine and within minutes of an IVP he'd passed the offending kidney stone. She'd kept him overnight because as a hard-working farmer she'd known he would be out at dawn instead of resting as she'd advised. She'd been home and asleep when she'd got the call that he'd had a fatal heart attack in the early hours of the morning.

Then there had been Moira Blakely, who'd had a history of drug dependence after a back operation that hadn't delivered the results she'd been expecting. She, too, had been carrying too much weight, and although her blood pressure had been borderline there had been nothing to suggest she would be dead within hours of being admitted.

The list went on, but as far as Keiva could see she had made the correct diagnoses and done everything according to clinical guidelines.

She sat back in her chair and sighed. She had five hours ahead of her and all she wanted was her bed. A young child had drowned the day before, dead on arrival. The distraught parents' screams had still been ringing in her head as she'd signed the death certificate.

Sometimes she really hated her job.

Detective Liam Darcy drove into Karracullen in the late evening, the heat and flies so far having escaped him within the confines of his air-conditioned car.

He hadn't really wanted this assignment, but ever since he'd broken up with Linda he'd felt like he needed a change of scene. Karracullen hadn't exactly been on his list of must-visit-before-I-turn-thirty-five places, but it was far enough afield to take away the risk of running into his ex-girlfriend with her nine-to-five accountant on her arm.

The hospital was as unpretentious as country hospitals went, he thought. Although the population of the Karracullen district tipped over forty thousand, the public health system was strapped for cash and it certainly showed out here where the bureaucrats didn't visit.

He parked the car in the doctors' car park next to a car that had obviously seen better days and better mechanical services than it was now apparently receiving. He could see a pool of oil running a dark trail towards the uneven kerb and grimaced. Bush mechanics had a lot to answer for.

The reception desk and switchboard was manned by a grim-faced woman of indeterminate age who almost barked at him when he approached the desk.

'Yes?'

He reached into his breast pocket and took out his ID badge. 'Detective Darcy. I'm on official business.'

'Who do you want to see?' She peered at him from over the top of her thick-rimmed glasses.

He inspected his notebook and came to the first name on the list. 'Dr Keiva Truscott. Accident and Emergency.'

'You've come in the wrong door.' She pursed her lips and pointed back the way he'd come. 'Down there and turn left. You can't miss it.'

He pocketed his badge and walked back the way he'd come, hoping the first interviewee didn't have a chip on her shoulder a country mile wide. Sheesh! What was with women these days?

He pressed the emergency bell and waited for someone to appear at the window. After about thirty seconds a woman in her late thirties appeared with a welcoming smile on her face.

'Can I help you, sir?'

He held out his badge. 'Detective Darcy. I'm here to interview some staff members.'

'Who in particular would you like to speak to?'

He didn't need to check his notes, he could remember the name. 'Dr Keiva Truscott.'

'Will you excuse me just one minute?' she asked. 'I'll just check if she's free.'

He thrust his hands in his pockets and inspected the anti-smoking sign for a moment or two, pleased he'd given up the habit years ago.

'She's with a patient.' The woman's face appeared at the window once more. 'Could you come back tomorrow?'

He took his hands out of his pockets and straightened to his full height. 'I'll wait.'

The woman gave him a wavering smile and disappeared from the window once more. A few moments later she was back with instructions for him to wait in the doctors' room down the hall.

'There's tea and coffee and sandwiches. Help yourself. Dr Truscott won't be too long.'

'Thank you.' Liam nodded and made his way down the corridor, the fragrance of brewed coffee pulling him like a magnet.

He pushed open the door marked DOCTORS ONLY and looked around. There were several comfortable chairs positioned around a square table, a small kitchenette to one side, where a pot of coffee was standing, a jar of sweet biscuits and a platter of sandwiches covered with plastic cling film. A collection of newspapers and magazines was scattered about as if someone had been called away in a hurry, leaving them open and shuffled, the slight breeze from the partially open window sending the sports supplement to the floor.

He poured himself a coffee and, scooping up the paper off the floor, spread it before him and examined the cricket score.

Keiva glanced at the clock as she wrote up the notes of her last patient for the evening.

'Where did you tell him to wait?' she asked Anne McFie, the ward clerk in A and E.

'The doctors' room.'

Keiva closed her notes and handed them to Anne. 'He's been waiting a while.' She lifted her hair off the back of her neck and groaned, 'Hell, I wish I didn't have to deal with this right now. I'm going to get the third degree when all I want is Channel Three and a Chinese take-away.'

'Best to get it over with,' Anne said. 'You've got nothing to hide. You're the best A and E doctor we've had here in years. Heaven knows how many others would have died without your skill.'

Keiva removed her stethoscope from around her neck and placed it on the desk. 'I don't know... Somehow the police have this habit of making everyone out to be a criminal. Even if you're not guilty, you feel it by the way they look at you.'

'I'm not sure that the detective will be looking at you quite that way.' Anne grinned. 'Did I tell you he's gorgeous?'

Keiva rolled her eyes as she shrugged herself out of her white coat. 'He's a cop. In my book that means he's looking for a scapegoat to make himself look good. Another case solved, another promotion.'

'He's just doing his job,' Anne said. 'Just like you.'

Keiva set her shoulders and turned for the door, schooling her features into clinical calm even though inside she felt like a naughty schoolgirl summoned to the principal's office.

She didn't bother knocking. She pushed the door open and

scanned the room with a sweeping look, her caramel gaze coming to rest on the most handsome man she had ever seen.

It took all of her clinical training to disguise her start of surprise as the detective met her eyes and rose to his feet.

'Dr Truscott, I presume?' Liam held out a large hand, and with just the slightest hesitation she placed hers within it. His fingers were long and tanned and dry, not clammy and sticky but dry.

She swallowed as his grey-blue gaze meshed with hers. 'I'm Detective Liam Darcy from Forensics in Sydney.'

'I…' She cleared her throat. 'Pleased to meet you.'

'I'm sorry to bother you while you're at work, but there are a few questions I'd like to ask. I'm assuming Barry Conning has told you why I'm here?'

'Yes.' She reached for a chair and sat down, forcing herself to look relaxed and at ease. She noticed he waited until she was seated before taking the chair opposite.

'What can I do for you Detective…er…Darcy?'

He held her gaze for a fraction longer than she would have liked, his cool, assessing stare making her want to fidget in her chair.

'As you are now aware, the Medical Registration Board has received some complaints about some unexpected deaths in this hospital. Police Forensics has been asked to do an assessment. It's an unusual pattern of deaths. As you were the doctor who treated each of them on admission, I'm afraid we have to ask you some questions.'

'Fire away.' She injected confidence in her tone, although his manner did nothing to inspire it. She read arrogance in every line of his handsome face, the straight dark brows drawn slightly together as if in consideration of her viability as a witness, the lean, cleanly shaven chiselled jaw set, the line of his firm mouth hinting at a determined if not somewhat forceful personality. His dark hair was short but styled with some sort of hair product, which suggested he was a man who liked control of all things at all times. Even seated, his considerable height was obvious—she guessed at least a couple of inches over six feet, maybe even more.

'I take it you write clinical notes on every admission?' He interrupted her silent appraisal.

'Of course. That's standard clinical practice.'

'On your review of those notes, have you had cause to question your initial diagnosis on any of the cases?' he asked, his grey-blue gaze very direct.

'I've reviewed my notes several times in these cases and am confident my diagnoses were correct, and that I followed the appropriate procedure for each patient.'

Detective Darcy leaned back in his chair, one arm draped over the backrest as he surveyed her features. The casual pose revealed the holster beneath his suit jacket. She could see the menacing bulge of his gun and wondered why he'd thought it necessary to interview her armed to the hilt.

She shifted her gaze and encountered his cool, studied look. Doing her best not to appear intimidated, she sat back in her seat and waited for his next question.

It seemed an age before he spoke.

'Dr Truscott, did you know any of the patients in question personally?'

'This is a relatively small town, Detective. I had met two of them before.'

'What? Socially?'

'Yes.'

'So you recognised them as soon as they arrived in A and E?'

'Yes, of course I did. That's not uncommon here.'

'How well did you know them?' he asked. 'Could you recall their names or did you have to check the notes?'

'I knew their names.'

'Which patients were they?'

Keiva could feel her tension increasing at the rapid fire of pointed questions but refused to give him the satisfaction of seeing her composure cracking around the edges.

'Patrick Grafton was a cattleman from a property I'd visited once or twice with friends. He was well known about the place, having been in many times when his wife was ill. Moira Blakeley used to work in the supermarket. There are few people in Karracullen who didn't come into contact with her some time or other.'

'And the other three patients?' He opened his notebook and inspected the names printed there. 'James Fisher, Keith Henty and Robert Grundle. You weren't familiar with them?'

She shook her head. 'I had never seen any of them before they came in as patients.'

'Can you recall their presenting problems?'

'I…' She felt at a slight disadvantage without her notes in front of her, and had to concentrate for a moment to recall the details. 'James Fisher came in with severe abdominal pain. I diagnosed a ruptured appendix and he was scheduled for emergency surgery later that evening.'

The detective glanced at his notes before returning back to her with an unblinking stare. 'He had the surgery at eight-thirty and was in Recovery at nine-twenty. Did you see him again?'

'No… I was busy with a road accident victim, and anyway he was the surgeon's responsibility by that stage, not mine.'

'Were you surprised to hear he had a fatal heart attack during the early hours of the morning after his surgery?'

She compressed her lips for a moment. 'It was unusual. He was in considerable pain when he was admitted. I wouldn't have thought it was enough to trigger a heart problem, but…'

'But?'

Keiva shifted in her seat. 'It happens from time to time.'

'In twenty-eight-year-old males?' There was a hint of accusation in his question.

She met his level look with as much equanimity as she could muster. 'No one is immune to heart disease, Detective Darcy. Bad diet, stress and lack of exercise are all contributing factors, even in younger people, according to some recent studies. And Mr Fisher did have peritonitis and he was overweight.'

'And yet Mr Fisher showed no signs of heart disease on admission?'

'We weren't looking for it,' she said. 'He came in with acute abdominal pain so locating the cause of that was the first priority.'

He seemed to give her reply some consideration before moving on to his next question.

'What about Keith Henty? What can you recall about him?'

'Mr Henty was a fifty-five-year-old man with a deep laceration to his leg as a result of a brawl. His leg required stitching and we kept him overnight as his blood alcohol level would have been high.'

'How high?'

She returned his direct look with one of her own. 'He was drunk, Detective Darcy. Very drunk. As far as we knew, he wasn't driving so we weren't obliged to test his blood alcohol level.'

She thought she saw a flicker of amusement at the corner of his mouth but then wondered if she'd imagined it.

'No heart symptoms?' he asked.

'Not that I recall.' She let out a small breath. 'He was a difficult patient to treat.'

'In what way?'

'He was aggressive, loud, demanding. I'm sure you've met the type—the usual loud drunk. His leg was in a bad way but he kept on wanting to leave before we could stem the haemorrhage.'

'How did you manage to restrain him so he could be treated?'

'Well, since public funding to country hospitals doesn't quite stretch to supplying handcuffs to all emergency staff, I'm afraid we have to resort to other means.'

The flicker of amusement was back, this time reflected in his eyes as they rested on her. 'Such as?'

'We calmed him down by talking to him as well as administering a sedative. A quick jab and he was a new man.'

'He was a dead man in a matter of hours,' he commented wryly.

She ran her tongue over her lips and shifted her eyes from the force field of his. 'Yes…'

'What do you remember about Robert Grundle?' he asked after a slight pause.

'He came in after a tractor accident. The right side of his body had been crushed by the back wheel. He was semi-conscious on arrival and died post-operatively. We were all surprised he made it that far, to tell you the truth.'

'According to the post-mortem, he died of a cardiac arrest, not injuries sustained from an accident,' Detective Darcy said.

'He lost eight litres of blood, Detective, most of it ending up on the floor of the operating theatre. There aren't too many seventy-year-old hearts that can cope with that sort of blood loss,' she pointed out. 'He died of the after-effects of hypo-volaemic shock.'

The detective closed his notebook and gave her a vestige of a smile as he got to his feet. 'That will do for now, Dr Truscott. I think I'm starting to get the picture. Thank you for your time.'

Keiva rose from her chair on legs that were not as steady as she would have liked, and without bothering to offer her hand made her way towards the door.

'By the way, Dr Truscott…' His deep voice sounded from behind her.

Her hand froze on the doorknob and drawing in a prickly breath she slowly turned to face him.

He'd moved from around the other side of the table and was now leaning back against it, his legs crossed at the ankles, his hands resting on either side of him on the wooden surface.

'Yes?' She dragged her eyes away from the dark shadow of his gun.

His eyes ran over her in one sweeping, all-seeing glance before coming back to her face. 'I'd appreciate it if you didn't leave town without notifying me personally of your where-abouts.'

She stared at him, her mouth dropping open in shock. 'You surely don't think I'm in some way responsible for those deaths?'

He gave her an inscrutable look. 'I make it a policy never to make assessments until all the evidence is before me. But I would appreciate it if you'd co-operate by staying in town until I've finished my enquiries.'

'You're barking up the wrong tree, Detective.' She threw him a resentful look. 'It's my job to save lives, not destroy them.'

The grey-blue eyes hardened a fraction. 'It's my job to find out the truth, Dr Truscott, and I don't intend to leave Karracullen until I do.'

CHAPTER TWO

KEIVA stormed out of the doctors' room without a backward glance, incensed at the attitude lurking behind the detective's questions. She didn't see the staff anaesthetist until she almost cannoned into him as she turned the corner. Campbell Francis caught her by her upper arms to steady her, frowning down at her from beneath his bushy, unruly brows. 'Keiva, what's wrong? You look upset.'

She let out an angry breath and pointed back the way she'd come. 'I've just been subjected to a grilling by a visiting detective.'

Campbell let his hands drop away from her. 'I heard he was in town. Barry told me there was going to be some sort of inquiry. Surely he doesn't think you're responsible?'

'I was first on his list,' she informed him. 'Heaven knows who is next.'

'He'll have to interview everyone who came into contact with the patients, I suppose…' He rubbed his chin thoughtfully.

'That will include the catering and cleaning staff,' she said. 'By the time he gets through that list, as well as the nurses and ward clerks, he'll be here for weeks.'

'Do you have any idea who's responsible?' he asked.

She gave him a startled look. 'For God's sake, Campbell, no one's responsible. Surely you can't suspect anyone of foul play? This is Karracullen Base Hospital. We don't have serial killers lurking in the corridors.'

'All the same, Keiva, even you must admit five deaths from undiagnosed heart attacks in as many months borders on the unusual.'

'Unusual, yes, but not inexplicable.'

17

'Maybe.' He gave his watch a quick glance. 'I've got to go, I told Lana I would be home an hour ago.'

'How is she?' Keiva asked.

He gave a small shrug which she read as defeat. Ever since Lana, his wife, had been injured in a car accident, leaving her partially paralysed, Campbell had been struggling to support her as well as work the often long hours his job required.

'You know how it is.' He gave her a sad smile. 'Things are just not the same any more.'

Keiva put her hand on his arm, giving it a gentle squeeze of encouragement. 'Would it help if I came to visit this weekend? I'm rostered off so I could sit with her while you play a round of golf.'

'She'd like that,' he said. 'But only if you're sure.'

She smiled. 'Of course I'm sure. I haven't forgotten how good you two were to me when I first arrived. I don't know what I would have done without your hospitality for those first few lonely weeks.'

'It was our pleasure.' He smiled back. 'We were quite disappointed when you found somewhere else to live. How is the little cottage going? Done any more renovations?'

'I still have two rooms to paint but it's starting to look more and more like a home instead of a doss house.'

'Attagirl!' His worn face split into a grin. 'Sing out if you need a hand any time. I'd be happy to help.'

'Thanks, I'll keep you in mind when I can no longer get the lids of the paint tins open.' She gave him a cheeky smile as he lifted his hand in a wave and continued on his way down the corridor.

The car park was dark and deserted when she finally made her way outside, the warm night air hitting her like a stuffy blanket.

She saw an unmarked police car parked next to hers and stiffened.

'You're late leaving,' a voice said behind her.

Keiva swung around to see Hugh Methven, the senior physician, standing two cars away, his keys in hand preparatory to unlocking his flash car.

'Oh, hello, Hugh.' She sent him a quick smile, which didn't quite make the full distance to her eyes. 'So are you.'

Hugh's green eyes ran over her, lingering on the upthrust of her breasts before returning to her face. 'How did your interview go?'

'Interview? Oh, that… Fine.'

'Nasty business, this.' He jangled his keys as he came across to stand in front of her. 'Any idea who is to blame?'

'No, none at all.' She gave him a direct stare. 'Why is everybody on about blame? Don't tell me you're turning into a super-sleuth.'

He held her unblinking look with ease. 'I've narrowed it down to one or two potential culprits.'

'Oh, really?' Her expression was deliberately scathing. 'I didn't know you fancied yourself as a hotshot detective.'

'Physicians are hybrid investigators, Keiva, my love. Surely you know that?'

She ground her teeth behind her forced smile. 'There certainly seems to be a lot of guesswork involved. Not unlike a vet, I've always thought.'

Hugh's green eyes grew cold and the line of his thin mouth tightened. 'I'd be careful if I were you, Keiva. You seem to forget I'm on the country regional recruitment board. If there's a scandal, you'll be on your way back to the city before you can say ICU.'

'I'd be careful, too, Hugh. You know how long it took to find someone to do this locum while Neil Pickstaff is away on sabbatical. One phone call to tell them I'm being harassed, and you know what will happen. And don't think I wouldn't do it.'

'It wouldn't surprise me what you'd do, Dr Truscott,' he drawled. 'It wouldn't surprise me at all.'

Keiva wrenched open her door and got into the car without responding. She wound down the window for air and waited until he had driven off in his own car before starting it, not trusting herself to drive while she was so angry.

Her car coughed and spluttered and gave three or four grunts as if about to start, before stalling completely.

'Damn!' She gave the steering-wheel a thump with her clenched fist. 'Don't do this to me now!'

A shadow came across her window and she turned to see Detective Darcy standing beside her driver's door. He leaned down to look at her through the open window.

'Trouble?'

'Nothing I can't handle.' She turned back to the front and turned the key once more, but the sounds coming from under the bonnet were not promising.

'Want me to have a look?'

Keiva swivelled her head to look at him, wondering what it was about men that made them think they were the answer to every woman's problems.

'Thank you, but I'm actually all clued up on how to start a car. Normally I just put the key in here and turn and, hey, presto, the car starts.'

Liam took in her ruffled hair, petulant scowl and flashing, toffee-coloured eyes in silent amusement.

'So…' He hunkered down beside the door so that he was on a level with her. 'What's a nice girl like you doing in a car like this?'

She rolled her eyes at him. 'My other car is a limousine.'

His chuckle of laughter unravelled her tightly controlled mouth so it stretched into what could almost be termed a smile.

'Come on, out you get and let me have a look.' He opened the door for her.

She hesitated, not sure she wanted to be beholden to him in ny way. 'I can call roadside help.'

'And wait two hours for them to turn up?'

He had a point, she had to admit. It was well after ten and pitch dark. It would be no fun waiting for any length of time this late at night. She eased herself out of the seat, injecting her tone with just the right amount of insincerity. 'I hate to put you to any bother.'

He shrugged himself out of his jacket and handed it to her to hold. 'It's no bother. I used to have one of these models myself.'

Keiva stood to one side and tried not to notice the expensive cut of Liam's jacket in her hands, or the hint of spicy aftershave she could smell clinging to the fabric. She could even feel his residual body warmth as she held it against herself, making her wonder what it would feel like to have that lean but muscled body pressed close to hers...

The bonnet springing open rocked her out of her wayward thought pattern. She watched as he unfolded his length from her car, moving past her to prop the bonnet up and shine a small torch inside.

She followed him around to the front of her car. 'You guys are certainly prepared for any contingencies,' she observed with a touch of wryness.

He slanted a sideways glance her way and smiled. 'You'd better believe it.' He turned back to the engine and began poking and prodding, reminding her of Geoffrey Ellerton, one of the town's surgeons, his experienced hands sure and steady.

'Can you give it a try now?' he asked, without looking up from what he was doing.

'Sure.' She placed his jacket carefully over the back of the passenger seat before sliding into the driver's side and turning the key in the ignition. The engine choked like someone from the respiratory ward before finally turning over with a deep rumble of mechanical relief.

'Keep the fuel going,' he called out from under the bonnet.

Keiva pressed her foot to the floor and the car roared.

'Not that much,' he cautioned. 'Ease off... Yeah, that's it.'

He closed the bonnet and came round to her, wiping his hands on a snowy white handkerchief. 'That should get you home, but I'd get it checked as soon as you can. The air filter's choked.' He closed the door and pocketed the handkerchief. 'Do you want me to follow you to make sure you get home?'

'No… I'll be fine. Thank you.'

'No problem.'

Keiva felt nervous with him standing there watching her. She reached for her seat belt and attached it firmly before beginning to reverse out of the space.

'Dr Truscott.'

The car almost stalled when she applied the brakes, but she coaxed it back into life as she looked through her window at him. 'Yes?'

He reached into the car, his arm almost brushing her breasts as he turned on the headlights. 'You won't get far without these.'

She didn't release her breath until his arm was back out of the car. 'Thank you. I was getting around to it.'

In spite of the evening heat she wound up the window and, not trusting herself to look at him again, reversed out of the space and made her way to the exit.

She was about to turn left out of the hospital grounds when she caught sight of his suit jacket still draped over the passenger seat beside her.

'Damn!'

The powerful beam of headlights shone through her car from behind, just like a predatory jungle cat's eyes stalking her stealthily.

She snatched up the jacket and, leaving the car running, made her way to where his car had pulled up just behind hers.

His window slid down with a soft mechanical whirr.

'I knew there was something I forgot.' He took the jacket from her, his long fingers briefly touching hers.

Keiva pulled her hand away and stepped backwards. 'Have a good evening, Detective Darcy, and thanks again for your help.'

'My pleasure, Dr Truscott. Drive safely now, won't you?'

'I always do,' she said, and turning on her heel went back to her car.

A few minutes later she turned into her driveway and the sleek black car tailing her purred past and off into the darkness of the night.

Keiva had not long arrived at work in A and E the next morning when news came in of a high-speed motorcycle accident victim due to arrive at any minute. As soon as the ambulance arrived a code blue was called, signalling a medical emergency. Somehow she knew this was going to be a tough one, motorcycle accidents usually were. And out here in the country the hospital facilities were somewhat limited when it came to dealing with serious multiple injuries. Most victims had to be transferred to one of the larger city hospitals once they were stabilized, but it all took time. Valuable, crucial time.

The rush of adrenalin hit her as the doors opened, with the ambulance officers calling out the relevant information. 'Approximately twenty-five-year-old male involved in motorcycle accident. He was found thirty metres from the bike, which had struck a guide rail. He was unconscious with a GCS of seven, his helmet was off, the left thigh was angled at forty degrees and the fracture was compound. His pulse was 100 and BP 80 systolic. We put in a cannula and so far have run in two litres of saline. We bagged and masked him with 100 per cent oxygen. He's got a hard collar on and a Donway splint on his left leg. We put him on a spine board and brought him in. The time of the accident was about six a.m. We took about twenty minutes to stabilise him and the trip here took fifteen minutes.'

'Right,' Keiva said, pulling on some gloves. 'We'll take over from here. Jane, have you called Campbell?'

'He's still tied up with a case but Carol Duncan, the anaesthetic registrar, is on her way to fill in till he gets here,' Jane the senior nurse replied.

'Right—we're going to intubate him.' She turned to the senior resident on duty. 'John, stabilise his neck while I clear his airway with a Yanker sucker.'

Carol Duncan, a twenty-six-year-old and somewhat inexperienced anaesthetic registrar came through the door. 'What's going on?'

Keiva quickly filled her in before asking, 'Carol, can you and John intubate while I check the chest and get another IV in?'

'Sure,' Carol answered. 'But his face is badly smashed, it's going to be difficult.'

'Just try. He's cyanosed and shocked. John, make sure you keep that neck under control. There's a high chance, given the mechanism of injury, that it's fractured. Jane, help me with the IV—get me a 14-gauge cannula and some blood tubes for cross-match. Thanks. There, IV is in, run in 500 mls of normal saline, stat, and get me whatever O-negative blood we've got.'

'I'm having trouble seeing the cords, Keiva,' Carol said. 'The pharynx is bleeding and swollen. I can't intubate him. We're stuffed. I can't do it. He's dead without an airway.'

'Just calm down, Carol,' Keiva said, wishing Campbell were present instead of his registrar. 'It's swelling all the time and it's getting harder to ventilate him. We've got to do an emergency cricothyroidotomy. I'll do it. Move back, please.' She turned to Jane. 'Get me a scalpel and size 6 tracheostomy tube, stat. John, undo the hard collar but keep that neck stabilised. Carol, what's his BP?'

'Seventy systolic. He's badly shocked and getting worse.'

'Check the leg,' Keiva instructed. 'Is there any external bleeding? I'm doing his cric now—transverse incision at the cricothyroid membrane. Stab back with the scalpel, artery forceps spread the incision, size 6 tube in, blow up the cuff, connected to the O2. It's inflating OK. We've got an airway!'

'Well done, Keiva,' Campbell said as he came in. 'Stand aside, Carol,' he instructed his registrar. 'I'll bag him.'

'The leg's bleeding badly. I've tightened the traction on the splint and rebandaged the leg,' Jane said. 'The bleeding seems better controlled. BP's up to 90 systolic.'

'Better check the chest, Keiva—feels hard to ventilate,' Campbell said, looking concerned.

'Good air entry on the left,' Keiva informed him. 'Hyper-resonant and no air entry on the right, and bony crepitus all over the right chest. I'll feel his trachea before you put that collar back in place, John. It's deviated to the left. Look at the neck veins—they're grossly elevated. He's got a right tension. Jane, get me a couple of 14-gauge cannulas. Thanks. I'm doing a right needle thoracocentesis. Second intercostal space, right mid-clavicular line—puncture just above the top of the third rib.' There was a distinctive hissing sound. 'Got it—hear that pressure release. I'll put in a second needle then, Jane, set up for a proper chest tube. Any easier to ventilate, Campbell?'

'Heaps. That's markedly improved his ventilation. Good job, Keiva.'

'John, what's his pulse and BP?' Keiva asked.

'Pulse 100, BP 100. I've got pulse oximetry on—sats are 90 per cent.'

'Great,' Keiva said. 'John, strip off the rest of his clothing while I assess his neuro status. Jane, call for X-ray, and get ready to put in a nasogastric tube and urinary catheter. Also, get the number of Neurosurgery at the Royal in Sydney—I need to get this guy CT-scanned and into neurosurgical hands, as long as we can stabilise him. No response to voice or pain. Campbell, you haven't given any drugs?'

'No, nothing.'

'He's unresponsive, probably a GCS of less than 7. Jane, I've changed my mind about the NG tube. There's too much blood and we don't know he hasn't got a base of skull frac-ture—we could end up passing it intracranially. But there's no blood on his penis, the perineum isn't bruised. Prostrate is not high-riding and no rectal blood. John, put in his urinary cath-eter while I start the secondary survey. Obs, Jane?'

'Pulse 90, BP 110, sats 100 per cent.'

'Good, we're winning.' Keiva let a small breath of relief as she saw X-ray arrive. 'Thanks, Bob. I need a lateral C-spine, chest, pelvis and left thigh.'

While the X-rays were being taken, Jane handed Keiva the phone. 'Sir Peter Pimm from the Royal in Sydney.'

'Sir Peter? I didn't expect you on call for neurosurgery. We've got a twenty-five-year-old male, motorcycle accident. He has GCS 7, no localising signs, flail right chest, compound fracture left femur. He's in critical condition. We've successfully resuscitated him but he has facial and pharyngeal injuries, as well as his head injury. We had to do a cricothyroidotomy. Can you take him for neurosurgical management? We don't have CT-scanning here.'

'Sounds bad, Dr Truscott. Give him 200 mls of 20 per cent mannitol, get immediate helicopter transfer to the Royal, keep his BP and sats up and keep his CO_2 normal. Don't over-ventilate him, and we'll CT him and take over as soon as you can get him here.'

'Thanks, Sir Peter. We'll get him packaged and on his way.' She handed the phone back to Jane. 'Get Patient Flight on the phone—we need the rescue chopper immediately. Campbell, John, status?'

'Ventilation OK, sats OK,' Campbell informed her.

'Pulse 90, BP 110. Urinary catheter in and 200 mls of non-bloodstained urine.'

'I'm ready for the chest drain insertion, Keiva,' Jane said.

'Good, I'll wash and re-glove. Size 6 and non-powdered, please. We won't need a local anaesthetic. Betadine skin prep. Prepping the right chest wall, 5-centimetre incision over the sixth rib in the mid-axillary line. Size 20 intercostal tube, please, Jane. Remove the trocar. Large artery forceps, spread with blunt dissection over the top of the sixth rib in the fifth intercostal space. Puncture pleura, spread with forceps. Tube inserted towards the apex, all holes inside the chest. Connect to the underwater-seal drain, Jane.'

'Bubbling and blowing, Keiva,' Jane informed her.

'Good. Sewing in the drain with size O black silk. Tape the tubing connectors, please, Jane, and take out the two thoracocentesis needles now we have the underwater drain in. I'm starting the secondary survey.'

By the time the flight team turned up the patient was stable but still not responding to stimulation.

Keiva watched as they loaded him and wondered what the outcome would be. Sometimes it was hard to bundle patients over to the next team.

Jane came to stand beside her. 'Somebody's son, somebody's brother,' she murmured sadly. 'That was textbook resus, Keiva.'

'Thanks, but I wish Campbell had been there right from the start. I don't think Carol has what it takes under pressure.' She turned to look at her friend and colleague. 'You all right?'

Jane nodded. 'I'll be fine.'

'It gets to all of us, Jane,' she said, disposing of her gloves. 'I know we're supposed to keep a clinical distance but, as you say, it's always somebody's loved one.'

Jane gave her a pointed look. 'How are you holding up over the inquiry?'

Keiva sat down and stretched her legs in front of her. 'I keep telling myself this is all a bad dream. I did everything by the book—you know how careful I am. But somehow I still feel guilty. Maybe I missed something.'

Jane gave her an incredulous look. 'Five times? Surely that's a bit harsh, especially for someone as highly trained as you.'

'No amount of training can remove the human element. Everyone has a bad day now and again and that's when mistakes are made.'

'Aren't you being a little hard on yourself?' Jane asked. 'You mostly work as a team with the A and E staff. Why should you take the blame?'

'The buck stops with me,' Keiva said resignedly. 'That's why my professional indemnity insurance premiums are as high as they are. One mistake and the weight of the law is on my back, not the nursing staff's, not the interns' or registrars', but mine.'

'You're making me glad I chose nursing instead of medicine.'

'Yeah, well, if you think that's going to exempt you from an interview with Detective Darcy, think again. Word has it he's intent on interviewing everyone from the grounds staff up.'

'How did it go?' Jane asked. 'I heard he singled you out last night.'

Keiva gave her a speaking glance. 'He was very direct.'

'He was good-looking, too, or so I heard.'

'If you have a thing for the tall, dark and handsome clone, yes, he more or less passes muster.'

'But he didn't get your heart racing, right?'

Keiva wondered what Jane would say if she told her just how fast her heart had been beating when his long arm had brushed past her to switch on her headlights.

'No… I'm in an anti-male phase right now. No amount of testosterone is going to nudge me out of it, I'm afraid.'

'You really shouldn't judge all men by your ex-fiancé's standards, you know. They're not all unfaithful creeps.'

Keiva got to her feet and pushed in her chair. 'So you keep telling me, but I've yet to be convinced. I'll see you later, I'm going to have my first hit of caffeine for the day and, as it is, it's three hours overdue.'

She made her way to the doctors' room, easing her hair out of the back of her shirt as she pushed open the door.

A tall figure turned to face her, his all-seeing gaze flicking over her before coming back to mesh with hers.

'Dr Truscott.' Liam held up the coffee percolator in his hand. 'Can I pour you a coffee?'

CHAPTER THREE

KEIVA seriously considered backing right out again but realised it would make him think she had something to hide.

She straightened her spine and entered the room. Taking the seat furthest away from him, she sat down.

'How do you have it?' he asked.

'Black.'

'No sugar?'

She shook her head and turned in her seat to face him. 'Am I interrupting your interrogations?'

He handed her the coffee, his eyes holding hers. 'I'm just about to get started.'

She took a sip of her coffee before asking, 'Who's first on your list today, Detective?'

'You've saved me a trip down to A and E to summon you.'

She put her cup down with a tiny betraying clatter of cup on saucer. 'You interviewed me yesterday. Surely you don't need to talk to me again?'

He opened his notebook. 'I'd like to hear a little bit more about your connection with Mr Grafton and Mrs Blakely.'

'Connection?'

'You said you knew them personally. I want to know how well and for how long.'

She blew out her breath. 'I've only been in Karracullen for about a year. I met Pat Grafton when his wife was admitted during the last stages of her terminal illness. He organised a fundraising barbeque for the palliative care ward and I attended with some friends.'

'Which friends?'

'Campbell Francis, the hospital anaesthetist, and his wife, Lana.'

'You boarded with them when you first arrived, is that correct?'

Keiva wondered who'd given him that information. 'Yes.'

'How did that arrangement come about?'

She frowned. 'I was staying at the hotel and Campbell offered to rent me a room.'

'His wife didn't mind?' His gaze was intent.

'Why should she mind?' She returned his penetrating look with a diamond sharp one of her own.

'Mrs Francis is in a wheelchair as a result of an accident. Is that correct?'

'Yes, but I hardly see what—'

'How convenient, then, for Dr Francis to invite a young, somewhat attractive woman to board with them,' he observed.

It was the 'somewhat attractive' that got to her. Although she knew *Vogue* or *Cosmopolitan* probably weren't going to be calling her any time soon for a photo shoot, she knew she had a good figure, clear skin and straight, even white teeth. 'Somewhat' attractive just didn't cut it with her.

'Lana Francis is a good friend of mine,' she informed him coldly.

He ignored her terse statement. 'How well do you know Campbell Francis?'

'He's a good anaesthetist.'

'I wasn't asking about his professional abilities,' he said. 'I want to know how well you know him.'

She sat back in her seat and deliberately took a slow sip of her coffee. 'I know he would never do anything to harm another human being.'

'You seem pretty sure about that.'

'Of course I'm sure.' She placed her cup on the saucer with another loud clatter. 'You should have seen him this morning. He did everything he could to help me save a young motorcycle accident victim. No one, but no one could ever think him capable of deliberately sabotaging lives.'

'So you think there's a possibility that someone has sabotaged lives in this hospital?'

She frowned, realising how he'd cleverly manipulated her into admitting there was a possibility of foul play.

'I don't know...' She stared at the dark dregs in her cup. 'I wouldn't have thought so but...'

'But?'

She returned her gaze to his. 'You're the detective. You tell me. What do you think?'

'It's too early in the investigation to say.'

She got to her feet and carried her cup to the sink, rinsing it under the tap before turning back to face him. 'I wish I could help you, Detective Darcy, but I've told you all I know.'

'If you think of anything, please, don't hesitate to call me.' He handed her a card. 'I'm staying at the Bullock and Dray. I can be contacted on that mobile number or at the hotel.'

She pocketed the card and met his cool gaze. 'I hope you find your suspect soon.'

'It can't be soon enough,' he said.

She elevated one finely arched brow at him. 'You're not finding the country air to your liking, Detective?'

'Suffice it to say it's been unexpectedly cold so far.'

'It's thirty-eight degrees in the shade. Exactly what sort of climate are you used to?'

The corner of his mouth lifted in a semblance of a smile. 'How's your car?'

'Firing on all cylinders.' She gave him a sheepish look. 'Or at last count at least three.'

His smile she thought would outshine the lights in the main operating theatre.

'You should get it checked by a decent mechanic,' he said.

'The only mechanic in town has a criminal record,' she returned. 'There's absolutely nothing about him that's decent.'

His amused chuckle sent a shiver of reaction up her spine.

'Get back to your patients, Dr Truscott. If I need you, I'll call you.'

Keiva turned and left, not sure she wanted to be exposed any longer to his particular brand of charm.

Within minutes of her return to A and E all hell broke loose with the arrival of a screaming child and a distraught mother. Keiva caught the tail end of Jane's it's-going-to-be-one-of-those-days glance as she flashed past with some notes on another admission.

'What seems to be the problem?' Keiva gently ushered the sobbing mother and child into the nearest cubicle.

'Gemma dragged the kettle off the bench and it splashed all over her chest,' the mother cried. 'I only turned my back for a moment and—'

'Try not to worry,' Keiva reassured her, before turning to Jane who had returned from the ward clerk's office. 'We need some iced water on these burns and an IV line with pain relief. One milligram per kilogram of body weight pethidine.'

Within a short time the IV was in and the child's howling had decreased to a sobbing whimper as Keiva inspected the damage.

'What we've got here are superficial first-degree burns, which unfortunately cause a lot of pain but thankfully not much scarring. The thing we have to be careful with is infection. We'll dress the burns with SSD, an antibiotic ointment.' She smiled at the young mother. 'She's a lucky little girl. You did the right thing by bringing her in so quickly. She'll have to be admitted for a few days on a drip with fluids but she'll be fine in no time.' She turned to Jane. 'We'll admit this young lady under Geoffrey Ellerton. Can you get Anne to see to the admission forms?'

'Sure.' Jane parted the cubicle curtains and made her way to the front desk.

Keiva turned back to her patient. 'The pethidine will make her drowsy but that can only be a good thing right now.' She smiled at the mother. 'Do you have other children?'

'Two boys,' replied Gemma's mother.

'How old are they?'

'Seven and eight. Gemma will be four in five weeks.'

'She's a princess, isn't she?' Keiva brushed the damp hair off the small child's face and smiled.

'I feel so responsible...' The young woman gave her an agonised look. 'I should have been watching but the phone rang.'

'Don't be too hard on yourself. Kids and accidents go hand in hand. I sometimes wonder how any of us get to adulthood in one piece. Here's Jane back with some forms for you to fill in with her. I'll pop up to the ward a bit later to see how Gemma is doing.'

'Thank you, Doctor.' The woman gave her a tremulous smile.

Keiva was on her way back to her desk when Anne handed her a note.

'Hugh Methven called a few minutes ago when you were with the burns child. He told me to tell you to meet him later for a coffee.'

Keiva gave the note a cursory look before scrunching it up and tossing it in the nearest bin. 'I hope you told him to get lost.'

'He was fairly insistent,' Anne said grimly.

'Only because he has no idea of the meaning of no. Hell, he's such a pain.'

Anne put her finger to her lips in a shushing gesture. 'We all know what he's like, but be careful, Keiva. You know how the hospital hierarchy works. Hugh's on the board of management. He'd think nothing of dispensing with your services if the mood takes him.'

'I'd like to see him try,' she bit out.

'Yeah, well, maybe your detective's enquiries are all about him doing exactly that.'

'What do you mean?' Keiva frowned. 'You think Hugh's behind this blame game?'

Anne gave her a level look. 'I wouldn't put it past him. He

likes a bit of mud to be slung around occasionally, as long as none of it sticks to him.'

'Well, none of it's going to stick to me either if I can help it,' she said determinedly as she opened the drawer of her desk to retrieve her purse. 'Will you page me if anyone needs me? I'm going to buy some chocolate. Somehow caffeine isn't doing it for me just now.'

Anne smiled and waved her off. 'I wish I could eat the amount of chocolate you do and still have your figure. How do you get away with it?'

Keiva gave her an answering smile. 'It's probably going to catch up with me one day, but until then I'm going to make the most of it.'

'Good for you.'

The cafeteria line was long so Keiva did a quick detour to the second floor where a coffee and confectionery machine was located outside the medical wing.

She placed the necessary coins in the slot and pressed her selection, but apart from the rattle of change nothing else happened.

'Damn it!' She thumped the side of the machine but it still didn't release her chocolate bar.

'Trouble?' a deep, instantly recognisable voice said from behind her.

She turned around to see Detective Darcy approaching, his dark-suited tall figure giving him a commanding presence in the narrow corridor.

'I don't suppose your mechanical expertise stretches to confectionery machines?' she asked. 'This one is refusing to give me my daily dose of chocolate.'

Liam ran his eyes over her slightly flustered appearance and privately wondered how she got away with a daily dose of chocolate without it showing somewhere on her person. She was slim to the point of thin, although her breasts were high and firm and her smooth skin translucent with good health. She didn't look like the junk-food type but, then, he reminded himself, she didn't look like a murderer either, but who could be sure?

'Let me take a look,' he said, and stood beside her.

Keiva felt the brush of his suit jacket along the bare skin of her arm and surreptitiously stepped to one side.

She watched as he dug in his pocket for some coins, his trousers stretching to accommodate his hand.

'Have you got another dollar?'

Keiva flicked her eyes up to his before she began fumbling in her purse for the coin. She handed it to him, trying to stop her fingers coming into contact with the smooth but masculine skin of his palm.

'Thanks.' He turned back to the machine and inserted the coin. 'Which one do you want?'

'Cherry Ripe.'

He pressed the button and the bar tumbled out into the dispenser at the bottom. He bent to retrieve it and, turning, handed it to her. 'One Cherry Ripe.'

The glance she gave him as she took the bar was tinged with embarrassment. 'Thank you.'

There was a funny little silence.

'What time do you finish your shift?' he asked.

Her eyes skittered away from his. 'I really don't think—'

'I have one or two questions I'd like to put to you.'

'I see.' She felt the colour run up her neck at her too hasty assumption about his motive for asking what time she finished work. 'I finish at eight.'

'What if I meet you in the doctors' room at ten past? Will that be convenient for you?'

'Fine,' she said, and pocketed her chocolate. She shifted her weight to one foot and then the other, feeling more and more like a reprimanded schoolgirl by the minute. She checked her watch, 'I'd better get back to A and E.'

He stepped aside for her to pass. 'I'll see you later.'

She gave him a nod and began to walk down the corridor.

One of the junior nurses came rushing out of one of the single-bed wards, her face flushed and angry, her eyes glistening with imminent tears.

'Meggie?' Keiva touched her on the arm and turned her to face her. 'What's wrong? Are you OK?'

Meggie gave her a stormy look. 'Dr Methven is an arrogant jerk. He just made me look like a complete idiot in front of a patient.'

Keiva gave a sigh and escorted her a little further along the corridor, doing her best to reassure her as they went. 'I know he can be difficult to work with, but try not to take it personally. Men like Hugh Methven are a dime a dozen in hospitals all over the world, not just out here in Karracullen, more's the pity.'

'How do you stand it?' Meggie stopped to look at her. 'I know you've had a few run-ins with him.'

'I'm not the only one,' Keiva told her. 'Just about every new staff member has to negotiate their way through the minefield of Hugh's manner. But as difficult as he is, he is still a very good physician and that really is the most important thing. Just do your best and in time he'll find someone else to pick on. Trust me, he always does.'

'Ah, Keiva, just the person I was hoping to see,' Hugh's voice said from further down the corridor.

'You were right, Keiva,' Meggie said in an undertone, her expression wry. 'Looks like he's just found his next target!'

Keiva turned as Meggie hurried off down the corridor and stretched her mouth into a cool smile. 'What did you want to see me about, Hugh?'

Hugh's eyes flicked over her, his thin mouth bordering on a smirk. 'You and the detective seem to be rather chummy. Two interviews in two days, or so I've heard. Are you helping him with his enquiries?'

'Aren't we all?' she asked.

'Has he told you of his findings so far?'

'No, and he probably won't, for the simple reason that there will be no findings, as you put it.'

'You sound very confident.'

Keiva dearly wished she felt it. 'Of course I am. I diagnosed and treated each one of those patients appropriately.'

'What will you do if the local paper gets wind of this inquiry?' he asked.

She swallowed the sudden restriction in her throat at the thought of the press getting involved. She'd seen firsthand what the media had done to her father when a patient had unexpectedly died under his care. The grieving family had pointed the finger of blame at him and the media had crucified him. Although the inquest had declared he had in no way been responsible, and the family's claim for damages had been dismissed, the mud had stuck and in the end had dragged him down so far he had never felt able to return to full-time work. When he'd died of a heart attack a short time after the inquest had closed, Keiva had had no doubt it had been brought on by the stress he'd been under for so long. He'd been dead ten years and yet the tight knot of pain deep inside her hadn't eased a bit. The local rag was small fry compared to the national broadsheets, but she knew it still could make things very difficult for her if she was named as primary suspect in a malpractice suit, let alone a multiple murder trial.

'I don't see why the press has to be informed,' she said. 'This is supposed to be an inquiry, not a witch hunt.'

'Tell me, Keiva.' His voice dropped to a conspiratorial undertone as he leaned towards her. 'Who do you think is responsible?'

She felt herself shrinking back to avoid the fetor of his forty-a-day smoking habit as his breath wafted over her face. 'I don't think anyone is responsible. I think it's simply what it is: an unusual pattern of deaths.' She made to move past him. 'Now, if you'll excuse me, Hugh, I have to get back to A and E.'

'Ever the dedicated little emergency doctor,' he drawled.

She gave him a cold look as she moved past. 'You'd better believe it.'

On the way back to A and E she received a page from Jane, informing her that an elderly man with chest pains had just arrived. She rushed back to the department and met Jane outside the cubicle. 'This is Mr Jeremy Holt, seventy-nine. He's had chest pains on and off all morning.'

Keiva entered the cubicle and, after greeting the patient, quickly began issuing instructions. 'John, hook him up to the ECG monitor. I'm putting in a drip and taking blood for cardiac enzymes.' She turned back to the old man and gave him a reassuring smile. 'Don't worry, Mr Holt. We'll have you sorted out in no time. How long have you been feeling unwell?'

The elderly man gave her a fragmented history, going off at tangents to tell her about his life on his small farming property out at Brackley's Gully. Keiva smiled politely and tried repeatedly to get him back on track so she could properly assess him.

'Do you live alone, Mr Holt?'

'Yes, my wife died three years back now. She used to be always at me to eat properly but now she's gone I don't go to much bother. Too much washing up when you cook. Not worth the effort for one person.' He grimaced as Keiva shifted her stethoscope on his chest. 'You live alone, Doctor?'

'I do, as a matter of fact.' She pulled the earpieces of the stethoscope out of her ears. 'We'll have to keep you in under observation, Mr Holt.' She patted his hand reassuringly. 'It looks like you've had a very mild heart attack, nothing to be too worried about given your history, but just to be on the safe side we'll put you in the coronary care unit for twenty-four hours or so. Dr Hugh Methven will be your physician and will oversee your care from here, on the medical ward.'

'Thank you, Doctor.' Jerry Holt held out a gnarled, work-roughened hand. 'If ever you're out at the Gully, drop in and see my place. It's not flash but it's home. I've lived there all my life.'

'I'll keep that in mind,' Keiva promised as she shook his hand. 'Now, here comes Nathan, our trolley man. He'll take you upstairs once your blood test results come back.'

'Bloods have gone off to Pathology. Here's the ECG, Keiva.' Jane twitched aside the cubicle curtain and handed it to her. 'And Campbell is on line three. Will I tell him to call back?'

Keiva clipped the test results to the patient's chart, noting the worrying ST elevation of myocardial infarction. 'No, I'll take it.' She handed the clipboard to the trolley man and turned to smile at Mr Holt. 'Take care of yourself, Mr Holt.'

'Thank you again, Doctor. I feel better already for seeing such a pretty face.'

She patted his leg on the way past and, still smiling, picked up the telephone extension at her desk. 'Keiva Truscott.'

'You sound happy,' Campbell said.

She pulled out her chair to sit down. 'I just attended to the loveliest old man.' She kicked off one shoe and wriggled her toes. 'What is it about men that they can still flirt with the ladies at close to eighty years old?'

Campbell gave a rough snort. 'Silly old fool. Who was it?'

'Jerry Holt. I thought he was sweet,' she said. 'Now, what can I do for you?'

'Lana wanted me to confirm your visit on the weekend. Are you still all right for Saturday?'

'Sure, I'm looking forward to it.'

'Great, so is she.' There was the sound of his pager going off. 'Must dash. Hugh is on my back about a patient. He's been developing rather a god complex of late, don't you think? I've had one of the nurses on ward four threaten to go out on stress leave because of his pestering. I'm tossing up whether to speak to Barry Conning about him.'

Keiva wasn't sure how to answer. Her professional standards insisted she didn't get caught up in workplace power games but even she had to admit Hugh Methven had become unbearable of late.

'He's all right in small doses,' she said instead. 'You just have to know how to handle him.'

'I'd be careful around him, Keiva. Don't forget what I told you when you first arrived. He has a bit of a reputation where women are concerned,' Campbell warned in a fatherly manner.

'I think I can safely say I will continue to resist the temptation of becoming involved with him,' she replied with undisguised sarcasm.

Campbell chuckled. 'You're a tonic, Keiva, do you know that? They should have you on prescription as a mood enhancer.'

Keiva smiled as she replaced the receiver a moment or two later. Campbell never failed to lift her spirits; she really didn't know how she would have survived this long in Karacullen without his and Lana's support. They were almost like a surrogate family to her.

An hour and a half later she had just finished stitching a leg wound on a teenager who'd injured himself at a football match when a code blue sounded, indicating a cardiac arrest upstairs on the wards. As part of the cardiac arrest team, she, along with Campbell and Hugh, was responsible for acute resuscitation in the event of a cardio-respiratory arrest anywhere in the hospital.

She rushed upstairs to the coronary care unit where Hugh and Campbell, with Carol Duncan at his side, were already in attendance at the bedside of Jerry Holt. Carol had inserted an IV while Campbell set up a giving set to take bloods and Hugh oversaw the management.

'Set up a lignocaine infusion,' Hugh said urgently as he watched the monitor. 'He's in VT.'

Campbell connected a side line to the IV set, but frowned. 'The IV has tissued. This cannula is too small, Carol. The peripheral veins are now collapsed. It'll be a real fiddle, getting another IV line in.'

'Put a central IV line in his neck,' Keiva suggested, her own heart racing at the erratic lines showing up on the monitor.

Campbell abandoned the patient's arm and within moments had a right jugular line in. 'We've got IV access again.'

The monitor's beeping changed to a high-pitched whine and Keiva watched in shock as a single flat line appeared, and then returned to ventricular tachycardia.

'We'll have to cardiovert him.' She snatched up the paddles as Hugh activated the machine. She placed them on Jerry Holt's chest but after the elderly man's frail body bucked beneath the charge, the monitor trace remained flat.

'Asystole. Intravenous adrenalin, stat.' Hugh took over, almost pushing Keiva out of the way.

She stood back as he administered the drug but there was no cardiac response. The monitor whined ominously above their heads, signalling time was running out.

'Start external cardiac massage. We'll have to give him intracardiac adrenalin,' Campbell said, 'bagging the patient with high flow oxygen between Keiva's external chest compressions.'

'Give me an ampoule of adrenalin with a spinal needle attached,' Hugh commanded urgently. 'The last thing we need here is another death.'

Keiva swallowed the lump of panic blocking her throat and watched as Hugh injected the adrenalin directly into Jerry Holt's heart.

The room became silent except for the whine of the monitor. After five more minutes of resuscitation, Keiva's hands dropped silently to her sides, her shoulders slumping in defeat as Hugh reached to turn off the machine.

'He's gone,' he said.

Carol made a choked sound from somewhere behind Keiva but she didn't turn around to comfort her.

She stood staring at the frail old man on the bed, his lined face now peaceful when less than two hours ago it had been smiling at her.

The sound of someone drawing the curtain around the bed and the formalities being announced jerked her out of her frozen state. She stepped back from the bed and mechanically removed her gloves, dropping them into the bin at her feet.

Hugh touched her on the arm as she made to go past. 'We did all we could, Keiva. Sometimes it just isn't enough.'

She stepped away from him, her expression grim. 'Maybe you could tell that to Detective Darcy. I'm sure he's going to want some sort of explanation.' She turned and walked out of the room, glancing at the clock on the wall as she left the ward. She was already twenty minutes late for her appointment with the detective. What was she going to say to him when she finally got there?

CHAPTER FOUR

LIAM glanced at his watch for the fourth time and began to drum his fingers on the table, but just when he decided to arrange for one of the hospital staff to page Keiva, there was the sound of female footsteps in the corridor and the door was pushed open.

'Sorry I'm late.' Her voice was slightly breathless. 'We had a…an emergency on the ward.'

Liam got to his feet as she approached the table where the chairs were gathered and, reaching across, pulled one out for her to sit down. 'No problem. I understand. Both of my parents are doctors.'

Keiva glanced up at him in surprise. 'Are they?'

He gave a nod as he took the seat opposite. 'My father's an endocrinologist in Brisbane and my mother is an obstetrician.' He gave her a small wry smile and added, 'It made for an interesting childhood.'

She gave him an answering smile. 'I can imagine.'

She noticed his eyes flick down to his notes before returning to hers. 'Your father was a doctor, I understand.'

It was hard to disguise her disquiet. Had he had her background investigated?

'I… Yes, he was.'

'He's retired?'

She gave him a direct look. 'He's dead.'

He didn't bother with the usual niceties, she noticed. No 'I'm sorry to hear that' or 'that must have been hard'. Instead, he asked, 'What about your mother?'

She lifted her chin a fraction. 'I haven't seen my mother in twenty years. She left when I was ten.'

His eyes were steady on hers. 'I see.'

43

Keiva was starting to feel distinctly uncomfortable. No one, but no one talked to her about her mother's desertion when she'd been a child.

'What's all this about, Detective?' she asked, somewhat sharply. 'I hardly see what my family details have to do with this investigation of yours.'

He leaned back in his chair in an almost indolent manner. Keiva found herself having difficulty reining in her temper at his cool treatment. She tightened her hands in her lap and silently seethed.

'You seem on edge, Dr Truscott,' he observed. 'Is there something wrong?'

'Wrong?' She glared at him. 'What could possibly be wrong? You think I'm a serial killer but, hey, all in a day's work, right?'

'I don't recall communicating my personal views on this case,' he answered evenly.

'You don't have to,' she shot back. 'I can see it in your eyes. You think I don't know what you've been up to? Digging around in my background for something to snatch up as evidence so you can get your next promotion?' She got to her feet and shoved the chair she'd been sitting on back under the table. 'Ask me whatever questions you like about my work and professional standards but as to my personal life—back off!' She gave the back of the chair a rough push and swung away for the door as tears started in her eyes.

Her hand was on the door when his voice sounded behind her in a low but no less commanding tone. 'Sit down, Dr Truscott. I haven't finished talking to you.'

She sucked in a furious breath and, giving him one last furious look, pushed the door even wider. 'Go to hell, Detective Darcy.'

The force of her exit left the door swinging for several seconds, the rush of air disturbing the pile of scattered newspapers on the table in front of him. Liam picked up the section with births, deaths and marriages and stared at the list of heartfelt messages for a few minutes before putting it back down amongst the disordered pile.

He got to his feet, and hooking up his jacket from the back of the chair walked to the door. Giving the room one last glance, he closed it softly behind him.

Keiva drove back to her cottage through a veil of tears. She was furious with herself for caving in to an emotional response she normally had under good control, but the death on the ward, on top of the detective's probing questions, had finally tipped her over the edge.

After she'd calmed down a bit she began to feel increasingly worried about the way Detective Darcy would interpret her behaviour, no doubt reading it as guilt. The very same thing had happened to her father. It didn't matter how many times he'd protested his innocence, the constant hounding had made him feel like a criminal. The suspicious, furtive glances, the innuendos, the speculation and gossip had all taken their toll.

She tossed her work clothes to one side and put on the cotton trousers and stained shirt she used for decorating, determined to work off her agitation by stripping the faded wallpaper off the spare bedroom walls.

Half an hour in and with the minor casualties of three finger-nails to show for her efforts, she stepped back and inspected her work. Just then the doorbell sounded and brushing her hair out of her face with the back of her hand she made her way to answer it.

Assuming it was Anne or Jane, who often popped around after work on a Friday, she opened the door to find Detective Darcy standing on the doorstep with a bottle-shaped brown paper bag in one hand. He had changed out of his suit and was dressed in a black T-shirt and jeans, his dark, still damp hair showing the neat grooves of a recent comb.

'Oh,' she said.

The corner of his mouth quirked at her one-word greeting, and he held up the brown paper bag. 'Are you off duty?'

She crossed her arms over her chest and gave him a pointed look. 'Are you?'

He smiled one of his thousand-watt smiles and something turned over deep in her belly. 'No more questions, just for tonight. OK?' he said.

She pursed her lips as if deciding whether to believe him or not.

'Come on, Keiva.' Her name tripped off his tongue like honey off a hot spoon. 'I was hard on you this evening and I want to apologise. I heard you had another death. I'm sorry, you must have been upset.'

She stepped back from the door to let him in, her expression still wary. 'Apology accepted.'

He stooped slightly as he came in, his height instantly shrinking the small hallway. He looked around at the new paintwork with approval. 'Nice job.' He glanced down at her. 'Did you do it yourself?'

'Yes.' She dusted her hands on the side of her thighs. 'I find it therapeutic.'

He handed her the bottle of wine. 'I was trying to work out if you were a red or white person. In the end I chose a Pinot noir.'

She took the wine from him with a twisted little smile. 'Hedging your bets, Detective?'

'Liam,' he said. 'Yes, you could say that. I try not to make any assumptions until I have all the evidence at hand.'

He followed her into the small kitchen and watched as she took out a corkscrew. 'Want me to do that for you?' he asked.

'I'll be fine,' she said, and began to cut the foil with the end of the corkscrew device. 'There are glasses in that cupboard above your head. At least you don't have to stand on a chair to get them.'

He took the glasses out of the cupboard she indicated and set them on the bench. Keiva was still battling with the cork but doing her best to hide it. She'd pulled heaven knew how many corks out of bottles—why the difficulty now with those steady eyes watching?

'Having some trouble?' he asked in exactly the same tone he'd used previously.

She gave the cork a tug but it remained firm. She let out her breath in a sigh of frustration and handed the bottle to him. 'Go on, you do it. Mechanical objects and I seem to be a bad mix at the moment.'

He popped the cork with effortless ease and poured two glasses, handing her one. He lifted his in a toast, that same bone-melting smile still playing around his mouth. 'What shall we drink to?'

She met his eyes across the top of their glasses, 'To no further questions.'

'No further questions.' He chinked his glass against hers and lifted the wine to his mouth.

Keiva took a hesitant sip, letting her taste buds experiment with the slightly tangy taste of the wine.

'How long have you had this place?' he asked.

'That's a question,' she said, and took another sip of her drink.

He elevated one brow at her. 'You drive a hard bargain. Am I not allowed any type of question?'

She pretended to give it some thought. 'Only if they're not too personal.'

'You don't like personal questions?'

'Not unless they're relevant to the topic being discussed.'

'What would you like to discuss?' he asked, and then laughed as he realised his mistake. He held up his hand in surrender. 'OK, I admit it. I'm full of questions. Must be an occupational hazard I guess.'

Keiva decided to ask a few questions of her own. 'How long have you been in Forensics?'

'Eight years. I started out in Accident Investigation and then I decided to do a Bachelor of Science followed by a Master of Medical Science. I guess my parent's influence won through in the end. Although I swore I'd never be a doctor, I found the science of medicine intriguing.' He took another sip of his wine. 'What about you? Was it more or less expected that you'd follow in your father's footsteps?'

'I don't recall any direct pressure to do so,' she said. 'I just wanted to help people, so medicine seemed the obvious choice.'

'And the move to the country?' he asked. 'Was that part of the desire to help?'

A small sigh escaped before she could stop it, 'No…not really. I was engaged. It didn't work out.'

'A medical colleague?'

She met his eyes once more. 'I thought having a partner who understood the demands of my career would guarantee a happy future. I was wrong.'

'It doesn't always work that way,' he said.

'What about you, Det— I mean Liam, is there someone waiting for you back in Sydney?'

He appeared to hesitate before answering, 'No. Not any more.'

Her eyebrows rose speculatively and he continued, 'My girlfriend grew tired of the irregular hours I work. We didn't part on the best of terms.'

'Too bad.'

He gave a dismissive shrug. 'I'm over it.'

'I envy you men,' Keiva said. 'You seem to be able to walk away from a relationship without a backward glance.'

'You think it's that easy?' he asked.

'Isn't it?'

He frowned and examined the contents of his glass for a moment. 'Not always.'

Keiva wondered what his ex-girlfriend was like and whether she realised how much she had hurt him. It felt a little strange to be seeing him as a real person instead of an officious police officer with an agenda, and yet somehow it made her soften her attitude towards him. She wondered if that was why he'd taken up this particular case, to get away and lick his wounds in private.

'Would you like something to eat?' she found herself asking, doing a quick mental tally of the contents of her refrigerator. 'I have some steaks…'

'I wouldn't want to put you to any bother.'

'No bother. I have to eat so fixing it for two is neither here nor there.'

'That would be great,' he said. 'The Bullock and Dray's menu isn't exactly haute cuisine, is it?'

She couldn't help a small laugh as she thought of the menu of artery-clogging food served there. 'No, I imagine not. Will you excuse me for a moment?' She indicated her renovating attire with a rueful grimace. 'I'd like to change. Help yourself to some mixed nuts in that jar on the bench.'

'Take your time,' he said as he pulled out one of the kitchen chairs and sat on it, his long legs taking up all the available space under the table.

Keiva went to her room and, closing the door softly behind her, tore off her rough clothes. She opened the wardrobe and peered at the contents in dismay. With Liam's 'somewhat' attractive comment still ringing in her ears, she rummaged through the rack to hunt for something a little more flattering than the trousers and shirts she usually wore at work. She only had two dresses and neither of them was currently in season, let alone fashion.

She closed the wardrobe in disgust, promising herself she'd drive the four hundred kilometres or so to Sydney at the next available opportunity to remedy her shortfall of clothes.

Her eyes fell upon her faded jeans slung over the back of a chair. Teamed with a pink T-shirt with silver sequins on the front, she knew it was about as feminine as she was going to get at short notice.

Once dressed, she examined her features in the mirror above her dressing table, grimacing at the speck of plaster dust on the upper curve of her cheek.

Hell, she needed a make-over.

She dragged a brush through her mid-length hair and fluffed it around her shoulders where it lay in soft chestnut curls. She ran her almost empty wand of mascara over her lashes and smoothed on a shiny lip gloss over the full curve of her mouth. She stood back and assessed her handiwork, twitching her lips from side to side as she deliberated over whether to apply perfume or not.

'Not.' She addressed the yellowed contents of the small crystal bottle Tim had given her, deciding it was high time she threw it out. She plucked it off the dressing table and, moving through to the bathroom, dropped it with a plop into the bin.

She dusted off her hands and made her way back to the kitchen.

Liam got to his feet as she re-entered the room. 'Can I top up your wine?'

'Sure.' She passed him her glass and met his eyes across the bench top. She saw a flicker of male interest as his gaze dipped to the sequinned front of her T-shirt where her breasts stretched the fabric.

His eyes came back to hers. 'You got rid of the plaster dust, I see.'

She gave him a reproving look as she picked up her glass. 'You should have told me.'

He smiled. 'I thought it looked cute.'

She could feel a hot blush creeping north from her neck and quickly turned to take out the steaks from the refrigerator. 'Is steak and salad OK with you?'

'Fine. Can I help?'

She placed some salad ingredients on the bench between them, carefully avoiding his eyes. 'You could toss these together, if you like.' She pushed a salad bowl towards him and a sharp knife for the tomatoes.

He set to work with the sort of quiet competence that suggested he was totally at ease in the kitchen, preparing food.

'Do you have any dressing?' he asked after a few minutes.

She went back to the fridge, turning the steaks on the way past, and handed him the low-fat dressing. He held it up and examined the label for a moment. 'So the lady who has a daily dose of chocolate worries about heart disease after all.'

Keiva couldn't help recalling Mr Holt's death earlier that day and turned away so he wouldn't pick up on her inner distress. He must have sensed something for she heard him put the bottle down and the sound of his footsteps as he came to where she was watching the steaks under the grill.

She felt his warm large hands come to rest on her shoulders, the pressure gentle but inescapable. 'I'm sorry, that was insensitive. Hugh Methven told me what happened this evening.'

She turned around to face him, 'That's all right. I should be used to it by now.'

His hands fell away from her shoulders but he didn't step away. Keiva could feel the warmth of his body this close. She could also see the way his eyelashes curled slightly at the ends, saw too the softer line of his usually firm mouth as he smiled at her wryly.

'You never get used to it, do you?' he asked.

She gave him a quizzical look even though she knew exactly what he was referring to.

'Death,' he elaborated. 'I can still remember the first body. The image never goes away.'

She let out a small sigh. 'I keep telling myself to toughen up, but each time it's like another piece of my stronghold is ripped away.' She stepped away and checked the steaks. 'I think kids are the worst. You don't expect to be pronouncing them dead. I don't think I'll ever get used to it.'

'I know what you mean. I've had too many in my time.'

She turned back to look at him. 'Your job must be so difficult at times.'

'It is, but, then, so is yours.'

'I know, but I get to do something to change people's lives. If I do everything right, they get a second chance.'

'That's true.' He let out a breath on the tail end of a sigh. 'I just get to pick up the pieces and deliver a report.'

She frowned as she turned back to the steaks. 'Have you come to any conclusions about this pattern of deaths you're so interested in?'

'Not as yet.'

She placed the cooked meat on two plates and handed him one as she turned around. 'So does that mean I'm still suspect number one?'

'I don't recall labelling you as such.'

She took her seat and when he sat down handed him the salad, her gaze on him.

'How did you find out where I live?' she asked.

'This is not a big town.' He handed the salad back once he'd helped himself. 'There are few people who wouldn't know where the pretty young Dr Truscott lives.'

'Pretty, huh?' She gave him an ironic glance. 'I thought your verdict was more along the lines of ''somewhat attractive''?'

His smile was lopsided as he reached for his wine. 'Did I say that?'

'You did.' She attacked her steak with her knife and fork as if it were him she was dissecting. 'You also implied I was having some sort of affair with Campbell Francis.'

He put his glass back down on the table. 'Listen, Keiva, some of the questions I have to ask during the course of an investigation may seem a little impertinent, but I'm afraid unless I peel away the layers I don't always get down to the truth.'

'I told you, Campbell and Lana Francis are my closest friends in Karracullen. I spend a great deal of time with them both socially and in particular with Campbell professionally.'

'And Hugh Methven?' he asked, looking at her intently.

She stabbed at a slice of cucumber with her fork without looking up. 'What about him?'

'Do you see him socially?'

She met his eyes briefly. 'Not if I can help it.'

He raised one dark brow speculatively. 'Not your favourite consultant?'

She took her time chewing the slice of cucumber, waiting until she'd swallowed it before answering. 'I try to avoid entanglements with men who have outsized egos. You could say I've been a little gun-shy since the break-up of my engagement.'

'You haven't had many dates out here?' he asked.

'I haven't had *any* dates out here,' she told him firmly. 'I'm only here for another two months so I don't see the point.'

'You're heading back to the city?'

She reached for her wine and surveyed his darkly handsome features for a lengthy moment. 'Don't you ever say anything without a question mark tagged on the end?'

He flashed his smile at her. 'I can't seem to help myself, can I?'

She rolled her eyes at him. 'There you go again.'

'Sorry. I'll behave myself. Tell me about your life here.'

'What do you want to know?' she asked.

'The usual stuff—what you do in your spare time, what hobbies you have, that sort of thing.'

'Well…' She toyed with her glass, one fingertip running round the rim. 'I've been doing up this place as a favour to the owner, who gave it to me rent-free while I do this locum. Apart from that, I like to swim in the gorge out at the river, go for long walks in the bush and generally chill out.'

'You're not tempted to stay on once the locum's finished?'

'I don't know…' She pushed her plate to one side. 'Sometimes I think I could make a life for myself out here, but then I think about all the things I love about the city. The beaches, the restaurants…'

'The traffic, the pollution, the crime,' he filled in.

'Yes, I suppose you're right,' she sighed. 'But then according to you, we have our own little crime wave going on out here.'

'So you don't think there's anything unusual about these deaths?'

She met his direct look across the table. 'I think they can be explained without having to conduct a criminal investigation, which could have devastating repercussions on this small community, not to mention the professional and personal lives of the medical staff involved.'

'That's what happened to your father, wasn't it?'

Keiva felt herself stiffen. 'You seem to know a lot about me, Detective Darcy. How about you answer one of my questions this time?'

'Fire away,' he said, leaning back in his chair.

'Have you had me investigated?'

Liam held her coruscating gaze with consummate ease. 'Does that worry you?'

She blew out her breath in an angry hiss. 'Why should I be worried? I've got nothing to hide.'

'Then what's the problem?'

'I don't like the thought of someone raking through the intimate details of my life without my permission, that's all.'

'I'd hardly call three traffic infringements intimate details.'

She flashed him a furious glare. 'What else did you find out? Where I used to live, who I used to date, even what size bra I take?'

His eyes were steady on hers as he delivered evenly, 'Jacaranda Crescent, Beecroft and Dr Timothy Perrington.'

She stared at him in a combination of shock and outrage. 'Don't stop there, Detective.' Her tone was laced with sarcasm. 'What about the third detail? If it wasn't on file, maybe you could use your widely acclaimed detection skills in hazarding a guess.'

His grey-blue eyes flicked to her heaving chest, lingering there a moment before returning to her flashing eyes.

'I think I'll wait until I've personally examined the evidence before I deliver my verdict,' he drawled.

CHAPTER FIVE

KEIVA was almost beyond speech. She scraped back her chair and snatching up the plates off the table, practically flung them in the sink, spinning around again to face him.

'I think it might be time for you to leave, Detective Darcy.'

Liam got to his feet and with indolent ease brought the rest of the things off the table to the bench beside the sink.

'Did you hear me?' She placed her hands on her hips in a don't-mess-with-me manner.

'I heard you,' he said.

'Well?' Her eyes challenged him.

'Before I go, why don't you tell me about the death that occurred this evening?' he suggested.

She set her mouth. 'Why ask me? Why don't you ask Hugh or Campbell?'

'You saw Mr Holt first.'

'I assessed him and sent him up to Coronary Care. End of story.'

'Not quite. You were present at his death an hour or so later.'

'I'm part of the cardiac arrest team. All three of us were present, as well as Campbell's registrar, Carol.'

'Was there anything unusual about Mr Holt's death?'

Keiva frowned. 'Look, Detective Darcy, he was close to eighty years old. He came in with chest pain and his ECG showed a recent myocardial infarct. I was more upset than surprised that he suffered a fatal cardiac arrest.'

'Why more upset than surprised?'

'He was a sweet old man…' She gave a barely audible sigh. 'He was lonely, his wife had died and he lived alone. I think he was glad to have a reason to come to hospital so he could have a chat with another human being.'

'You talked to him about his life while you were treating him?'

'Of course. Patients are people, their diseases don't stop them from being human, you know.'

'I didn't suggest they did,' he returned. 'How was his manner towards you?'

Her forehead furrowed as she looked back at him. 'How do you mean?'

'Was he polite, friendly or agitated or aggressive?'

'He was in a bit of pain but he wasn't really agitated in any way. He was friendly, maybe even a bit flirtatious.'

'Flirtatious?' He frowned down at her.

'Yes, lots of older men are.'

'Were any of the other patients you treated flirtatious towards you?'

'Which ones?' she asked.

'The ones who have subsequently died.'

Keiva was having trouble following his line of questioning. 'What are you trying to get at, Detective?' she asked pointedly. 'That I regularly dispense with any patient who is overly friendly with me?'

'Not at all. I'm just looking for a connection between the cases.'

'I fail to see any connection,' she said. 'Besides, aren't you forgetting Moira Blakely? She definitely didn't flirt with me.'

'What about Patrick Grafton? How was his manner towards you?'

Keiva pressed her lips together as she tried to recall the details of that day. 'He was in a lot of pain on admission. Renal colic can be worse than childbirth. He was very agitated, not his usual cheerful self at all.'

'Did he do or say anything out of the ordinary?'

Her expression grew thoughtful. 'No…not really, but…' She let her sentence trail away.

'But?' Liam Darcy's eyes pinned hers.

'I hadn't really thought about it till now…' Her forehead

creased in another deep frown. 'He grabbed my arm at one stage before I could administer the pethidine. I almost injected myself instead.'

'Who else was with you when this happened?'

'John Fielding, the senior resident, and Jane Catchpole, the nursing manager of A and E. Hugh Methven was there at one stage but only as he passed through to attend to another patient. And I'm pretty sure Carol Duncan, the anaesthetic registrar was hovering in the background as usual.'

'Anyone else?' he asked.

'I'm not sure…' She bit her lip as she tried to remember. 'I think there was a junior nurse helping someone to dress in the next cubicle, and a cleaner was floating around as someone had been sick in the reception area.'

'No one else?'

'I don't think so.' She looked at him in growing consternation. 'You surely don't think it's relevant, do you?'

He gave a slight shrug. 'Who knows? Sometimes the smallest, seemingly insignificant details are the ones that in the end will solve a mystery.'

'But I don't see how you can link all five deaths to someone. A heart attack isn't like a gunshot wound or a stabbing.'

'Heart attacks can be induced,' he pointed out.

Her expression grew serious as she considered the possibility. 'But that would mean someone administering a lethal drug of some sort. Not all that easy to do with a whole host of witnesses hanging about. This is a hospital, we have a strict code of practice when it comes to the administering of drugs. Every single pill or jab is written up and signed by two staff members. If even half a pill isn't accounted for, there is an incident report.'

'What if the drugs came from outside the hospital?'

'Illegal drugs, you mean?'

'Not necessarily. What if someone had a ready supply of some substance, say, a prescribed medication, for instance. A medication administered to someone in the wrong dose could prove to be dangerous, if not fatal,' he said.

'That's certainly possible but that would be taking a risk, surely? If there's an autopsy they'd never get away with it.'

'Only if the autopsy was ordered immediately. Some toxic substances don't last long in the body tissues. And autopsies are not routinely carried out in a hospital of this size, certainly not in the instance of a myocardial infarction.'

His words voiced Keiva's own thoughts and she looked up at him in wide-eyed alarm. 'It's a bit late for autopsies—all five patients have been buried.'

'Mr Holt hasn't.'

'You surely don't think…?' She swallowed deeply.

'I can't at this stage rule out the possibility that his death was hastened in some way.'

'What will you do? Order an autopsy?'

He nodded. 'I think it might be wise.'

'It all seems so unbelievable…' She reached for a chair and sat down heavily, staring at her hands as they held on to the table for support.

He took the other chair and, bringing it around, sat down next to her. He took one of her hands and squeezed it gently, his long fingers curling around her slender ones.

'Tell me about the other three patients. Let's go through them one by one, starting with James Fisher, the twenty-eight-year-old with appendicitis.'

Keiva stared down at their linked hands, wondering how it would feel to have those long tanned fingers scraping through the curtain of her hair, along the silky skin of her inner thigh…

'Keiva?'

She raised her eyes to his, her heart giving a funny little skip when she saw the intense look he was giving her. She ran her tongue over the dryness of her lips, watching as his eyes followed the movement before returning back to her troubled gaze.

'Tell me about James Fisher,' he repeated. 'Tell me everything, even if you don't think it's important.'

She slipped her hand out of his and used it to tuck a strand of hair behind her ear. 'James Fisher was in severe pain when he arrived. I suspected appendicitis and organised for an ultrasound of his abdomen. It was obvious from the ultrasound that the appendix had burst so I called for surgery for the first available opportunity. Geoffrey Ellerton was already in Theatre with another emergency so we had no choice but to wait. We administered appropriate pain relief and toughed it out until Geoffrey was free. When the operation was performed, peritonitis had already set in so his recovery was expected to be prolonged.'

'Was James at any time a difficult person to manage?'

'No... Considering his level of discomfort, he was polite and compliant at all times.'

'Do you remember anything of what he said to you?'

'Not much. We chatted about his girlfriend at one stage, you know, to sort of keep his mind off his pain. Then Carol came down from Theatre to do an anaesthetic assessment.'

'What did James say?'

'He told me he'd just broken up with his girlfriend. I commiserated with him and told him I knew how he felt as I had a broken relationship on my personal CV as well. He laughed and...'

'And?'

She looked at him once more, her expression clouded with increasing disquiet. 'He suggested we get together some time for a drink.'

'What did you say?'

'I didn't really get the chance to answer him as the trolley man arrived at that point to take him up to Theatre. I touched him on the shoulder and wished him well and he was wheeled out.'

'Was anyone with you the whole time you were treating James?'

'It's sort of hard to remember clearly,' she said. 'A and E is so busy at times and when I'm concentrating on a particular patient I don't really worry too much about who's in the background unless they're part of the immediate treatment team.'

'Just tell me who you do recall being there.'

'Jane was on leave so I had Fiona Trent, another nurse manager, instead. The radiographer on call was Corey Brock and the trolley man was Nathan Frost. Campbell came down to check Carol's assessment just before he was wheeled up to Theatre.'

Liam had taken out a notebook and was listing the names she gave him. Keiva watched as his handwriting ran across the page with a distinctively male script, efficient and authoritative.

His eyes met hers once more. 'Anyone else?'

She shook her head. 'I don't think so.'

'Let's move on to Keith Henty. Refresh my memory on him.'

'Mr Henty was difficult from the word go. His leg was badly lacerated and there was heavy bleeding, which was hard to control in his inebriated state.'

'You told me previously you administered a sedative.'

'Yes. Midazolam. He went from being verbally abusive to co-operative within minutes.'

Liam looked up from his notepad. 'How was he verbally abusive? What did he say?'

Keiva wondered if she should give him a slightly censored version but in the end gave it to him unabridged in all its offensive and colourful detail. She rattled off what she could remember of the vituperative phrases as if they were a regular feature of her vocabulary, noting as she did so that he didn't even flinch.

'You weren't offended by any of that?' he asked casually, glancing up from his notes.

She gave a little shrug. 'He was drunk. He wouldn't have remembered a word of it the next morning.'

'He certainly didn't, considering he was by that time well and truly dead,' Liam commented dryly.

Keiva caught her bottom lip with her teeth as the truth of his statement hit home.

'Who else heard this verbal abuse?' he asked after a short pause.

She gave him a wry look from beneath her lashes. 'Just about everybody in the hospital. Mr Henty may have had a dodgy heart but there was certainly nothing wrong with his lungs.'

A brief smile relaxed his features. 'Let's narrow it down to the witnesses in the room. Who was there with you?'

She told him the same names as previously, with the addition of Hugh Methven, who'd come in for added security.

'You were concerned about your safety?' he asked.

'Staff in A and E departments across the country are at risk of assault or injury when patients are out of control. Even if they're not drugged up or drunk, some can prove to be quite violent when pushed to the limit with pain. Some of the larger city hospitals now employ security guards to deal with the problem, particularly on Friday and Saturday nights when things are often escalated by the abuse of alcohol and drugs. We don't have security at Karracullen Base.'

'Yes, I'm aware of that.' He turned to a new page of his notebook and met her eyes once more. 'Let's go to Robert Grundle. What do you remember about his admission?'

She gave a ragged sigh as she brought the older man's features and injuries to mind. 'He was in a bad way when he came in. He was in and out of consciousness most of the time he was in A and E. By the time we got him up to Theatre he wasn't looking good.'

'Did he say anything to you or another member of staff in the time he was in A and E?'

'Not really, but when I was examining him he threw out an arm to ward me off. He was in a lot of pain, of course, and although we'd put in a drip and were giving him small boluses of IV pethidine, it wasn't doing much to mask it. He caught me on the shoulder and I would've fallen backwards except for Hugh.'

'What did Methven do?'

'He steadied me and then I went on with the examination. By this time Mr Grundle had lapsed into a coma.'

'You weren't hurt by his flailing arm?'

'Not at all. It just took me by surprise.'

'So there was no other exchange between the patient and you or anyone else?'

'No, within a few minutes he was being prepped for Theatre, but as I told you the other day, he had a cardiac arrest and died on the table.'

'Blood loss, didn't you say?'

She nodded. 'We couldn't keep the blood supply up. He'd already been through our whole supply of O-negative and type-specific blood. Further blood loss tipped him over the edge.'

Liam tapped his pen on the top of his notebook for a moment, as if mentally processing all she'd told him, his eyes still steady on hers.

'Do you still think there's some sort of connection?' she asked.

'I'm not sure, but I think it's worth documenting for closer inspection.'

'But what about Moira Blakely?' she asked. 'As far as I recall, nothing much was said when she came in. We all knew the routine—she was known as drug dependent following complications from back surgery. She came in so regularly it was like being on autopilot when we looked after her. We managed her pain and sent her to the ward for a few days.'

'At this point in time I will work on the more obvious connections before I search for the less apparent.' He got to his feet, putting his notepad and pen into his back pocket. 'If you think of anything else, let me know. And it goes without saying that if you see or hear anything of a suspicious nature, I want you to inform me immediately.'

Keiva rose to her feet, holding on to the back of her chair as she looked up at him. 'So am I to take it from this line of enquiry that I'm no longer suspect number one?'

He gave her an unreadable look. 'It could well be a coincidence that each of the patients you dealt with subsequently died, but I'm of the opinion that you are connected to this in some way.'

'How do you mean?'

'I haven't decided as yet.'

'So you haven't yet ruled me out?' She gave him a hardened look. 'Come on, Detective, surely you can see I'm totally innocent in all this? What possible motive could I have?'

'I'm still gathering evidence. I haven't yet come across possible motives.'

'I can't believe I'm hearing this.' She pushed herself away from the table with a harshly indrawn breath. 'This is ludicrous! I've done nothing wrong—*nothing*. How dare you come to my home and imply I'm responsible in some way for a series of deaths that in all probability have a perfectly natural explanation?'

'If there was a natural explanation that everyone was satisfied with, I wouldn't have been assigned to investigate this matter in the first place,' he said.

'So, in the absence of one, are you going to simply make something up to satisfy the powers that be? Is that how you'll get your next pay rise, Detective? By sucking up to the boss with yet another file stamped ''Solved'' across the front?'

Something flickered in his eyes as he surveyed her outraged expression, but she went on, regardless. 'I'm surprised you haven't leaked something to the press by now to up the stakes a bit. That's just what this town needs, a hint of a scandal to set the tongues wagging. Perfectly innocent people will have to face all the innuendo and the furtive glances but, hey, what does that matter when you'll be gone in a matter of weeks with a fat pay cheque tucked in your holster?'

'Are you quite finished?' he asked, a tiny nerve pulsing at

the side of his set mouth, the only visible sign of the somewhat tenuous hold he had on his temper.

'No, I'm not,' she answered, undaunted. 'I swear that if your stupid enquiries damage my professional reputation in any way whatsoever, I will be pursuing legal action. I won't take this lying down. I've worked too hard and too long to allow some blow-in to ride roughshod over my character and career.'

She hadn't noticed his movement towards her, so intent had she been on saying her piece. It was only when she'd stopped speaking that she realised there was very little space between them, his large body now blocking the only escape route between the table and the kitchen bench.

She sucked in a sharp little breath as his eyes pinned hers like laser beams, his lean jaw rigid with barely controlled anger.

'You know something, Dr Truscott?' His voice was velvet-encased steel. 'I'm a little tired of your uncooperative attitude in this inquiry. It kind of makes me wonder whether you're not the innocent do-gooder everyone assumes you to be.'

'I don't care what you think,' she spat back, furious with his insinuation.

'Don't you?' One of his dark brows rose in a perfect arc of cynicism.

'Not one little bit.' She glared back at him. 'Why don't you arrest me now?' She held out her wrists, challenging him with her flashing eyes. 'Go on. Think of how thrilled the boss will be. Another case solved by the brilliant Liam Darcy, the hot-shot city forensics detec—'

His hands suddenly came down around both her wrists exactly like a set of handcuffs, his long fingers curling around her slender bones in an inescapable hold as he tugged her towards him. She collided with the hard wall of his chest, all the air going out of her lungs as his eyes burned down into hers.

'I've a good mind to do exactly that,' he ground out darkly. 'Nothing would please me more than keeping you under close watch for a day or two.'

She found her voice at last, injecting as much venom into it as she could under the present heart-stopping circumstances. 'Don't let the law of the land stop you. It seems to me you don't mind acting outside it from time to time, holding me against my will like this.' She glanced down at her hands trapped in his and added as she looked back up at him, 'Isn't this commonly referred to as police brutality?'

'No.' He pulled her even closer, the hardened ridges of his very male body against her imprisoned hands shocking her into silence. 'This goes by a completely different name.'

Her eyes widened as she saw the naked intention in his glittering gaze, but before she could offer a single word of protest his mouth had swooped down and captured hers.

CHAPTER SIX

KEIVA had never been so unprepared for a kiss. Her startled gasp disappeared into the warm cave of his mouth as it commandeered hers, his firm lips taking control with devastating expertise. She felt the ramming of her heart against her ribcage as a thin ribbon of desire began unfurling from deep within her, totally surprising her with its intensity.

It had been well over a year since male lips had come into contact with hers, but there was little in her past experience to compare with the mastery of Liam's determined mouth as it ground against hers with burning intensity.

His tongue probed for entry and her stomach somersaulted as he achieved it, tasting her and teasing her into an intimate mating she hadn't thought possible a few days ago. She clung to him unashamedly, her legs weakening beneath her as his hard body pressed her from chest to quivering thigh, the unmistakable evidence of his maleness burning into her belly.

She felt his hands leave her wrists to slide up her body, one hand delving into her hair, his fingers threading through the silky strands as he held her face to his to gain better access to her trembling mouth. From the furthest reaches of her brain a tiny voice insisted she pull away, but even though her mind was willing her body was definitely not.

She realised that prior to this she had never really felt the full force of physical desire. She'd been physically intimate with her ex, Tim, but never had she felt the urgency she was experiencing in the arms of a man who, she reminded herself painfully, thought she was capable of murder.

The truth was sobering enough for her to freeze in his embrace. Sensing the change in her, he released her, stepping back from her so suddenly she felt herself teetering on legs that were not up to the task of keeping her upright.

He put some distance between them, his eyes seemingly reluctant to meet hers as he addressed her in stiff formal tones. 'I'll see myself out. Thank you for dinner.'

She couldn't think of a single thing to say and stared at his retreating back as he left the room. She heard the front door open and close, could even pick up the sound of his firm determined tread crunching on the gravel as he made his way to his car. She heard the roar of the engine and the squeal of tyres as he backed out of the driveway and then the slight slowing of the engine as he took the sharp bend at the end of the street. The sounds gradually faded into the distance and then and only then did she lift a shaky hand to her swollen mouth, running her fingertips over the sensitive curves with an almost tentative, exploratory touch.

Keiva received a call first thing on Saturday morning from Jack Portland, one of the A and E doctors, who asked if she could cover him for a couple of hours while he attended his son's tennis match. Fourteen-year-old David had won every match in the summer tournament so far and looked as if he had the potential to go a lot further.

Jack Portland had not long left A and E after briefing her on a couple of patients, when a call came through that an eighteen-year-old was being brought in after collapsing at an all-night party.

'It's Isaac Quentin,' Jane informed her. 'His friends are already here—they've beaten the ambulance.'

Keiva addressed the two young men and three girls who were hovering in the foyer, each of their faces white with fear.

'You five were with him when he collapsed? Tell me exactly what happened.'

One of the boys answered. 'Isaac was acting weird for a couple of hours, drunk-like, but he hardly ever drinks, maybe a light beer now and again. He had just the one drink, I'm pretty sure.'

'You mean he was falling over, slurring his speech, that sort of thing?' Keiva asked.

'Yeah, all of that and saying funny things, like he was confused.'

One of the girls added, 'Just before he collapsed it was like he couldn't tell who we were. You know, couldn't even recognise us.'

'What happened then?' Keiva asked.

'He was standing in the middle of the dance floor, sort of stumbling around more than dancing, then his eyes went all glassy and he fell down,' the taller of the two youths said.

'Yeah, and then he started shaking all over, like with an epileptic fit, frothing at the mouth.'

'He bit his tongue 'cos there was blood everywhere,' one of the girls put in.

'How long did the fit last?' Keiva addressed the girl who had just spoken.

'Not long…maybe a minute. Then he went all quiet…' She gave a choked sob. 'We thought he'd died…'

'Someone called for the ambulance and Jake and I rolled him onto his side and held his chin up like we learnt at Scouts,' the second boy told her.

'He's in the emergency bay, Keiva,' Jane informed her as she came in. 'The ambos have got oxygen on and the resident has got in a drip. He's deeply unconscious. You'd better come and take a look.'

'Thanks, Jane.' Keiva turned back to the patient's friends. 'Thanks guys. Stick around in the waiting room and I'll come out once I've seen him to let you know how he's doing.'

'He's got a GCS of 3, Keiva,' John told her as she came in to the emergency bay. 'I don't know what's wrong with him, but he's not responding to voice, touch or pain. I've got normal saline running in, and he's breathing spontaneously on O_2 with an airway in and a high-flow mask. His sats are 98 per cent. Could it be a drug overdose or spiked drink?'

'I don't think so, John,' she said. 'He'd go down in a few minutes if he was drugged. His friends said he was acting funny for a couple of hours and he only had one drink all night—and I believe them. Did you get bloods off when you put in the drip?'

'Yes, full screen. Results in forty-five minutes.'

'Good, but rather than wait, let's do blood gases on our machine here. Jane, do a pinprick blood sugar.'

'I'm onto the blood gases now,' John said.

'Look at this, Keiva,' Jane said. 'The blood sugar is off the top of the scale.'

'Keiva, the blood gases!' John said. 'Look at the result on the screen. He's got severe metabolic acidosis.'

'He's in ketoacidotic coma,' Keiva said. 'He's an undiagnosed diabetic. We'll need to set up an insulin infusion, push IV fluids hard, and get Hugh Methven in.'

'Here come the electrolytes,' John said, looking down at the results. 'Hell, his potassium is 5.8. That's dangerous—he could arrest.'

Keiva fought down the tidal wave of alarm that gushed through her. 'We'll need to get that down, but that should happen with the insulin and rehydration. Put on ECG dots, keep him monitored continuously and repeat his potassium tests in fifteen minutes after the insulin has brought down his blood sugar. Get in a urinary catheter, Jane, and set up an ICU bed.'

'Dr Methven's on the phone, Keiva,' John informed her. 'He'll be here in half an hour but wants to talk to you.'

Keiva stripped off her gloves and took the phone from him. 'Hugh, we've got an eighteen-year-old male undiagnosed diabetic in severe ketoacidosis.'

'Yes, John just told me. What are you doing for him?' Hugh asked.

'Insulin infusion, rehydration and monitoring his potassium, as well as airway care until he regains consciousness. He'll go up to ICU now.'

'Good work. I'll catch up with him there. By the way…' He paused for a second before continuing, 'It was nice of you to cover for Jack Portland. Enjoy the rest of your weekend.'

'Thanks…' Keiva hung up, wishing that Hugh would be as pleasant and easy to deal with all of the time instead of just occasionally. She really couldn't work him out.

'ECG dots are on, Keiva, but he's got a funny rhythm,' Jane said.

'Let's look at that… Yes, he's having Ventricular Ectopic Beats from the high potassium. Speed up the rate of the insulin infusion, John, and do another potassium now, and again when he's settled into ICU. Have the crash trolley at his bed until this settles down.'

'Will do,' John said.

Keiva rolled her shoulders to ease the build-up of tension once the patient had been transferred to ICU.

'David Portland had better have won that tennis match,' Jane said wryly as she began to clean up.

Keiva gave her a you-can-say-that-again look and moved to the door. 'I'd better let his friends know what's going on.'

The soft whirr of Lana's wheelchair could be heard as Keiva waited for the door of the Francises' house to be answered later that morning.

'Keiva, my dear.' Lana tilted her cheek for a kiss. 'How lovely to see you. Have you been busy? Campbell told me things have been rather stressful lately.'

Keiva gave her a rolled-eye look as she closed the door behind her. 'You wouldn't believe the week I've had.'

'Come into the morning room and tell me all about it.' Lana activated her chair in the direction of the room she'd indicated. 'I heard there's a forensics detective in town. Have you met him yet?'

Keiva wondered what her friend would say if she told her

that not only had she met him but been both interviewed and interrogated and finally kissed by him, all in the space of a couple of days.

'Once or twice,' she answered, avoiding direct eye contact.

'Word has it he's rather attractive,' Lana said.

Keiva gave a casual shrug and mentally clocked up a small victory of her own. 'Somewhat, I suppose.'

'Do you think there's anything in the speculation going around?' Lana asked. 'Campbell told me there's some concern over a series of deaths. An unusual pattern, I think he said. Do you think there's anything untoward going on?'

'I don't know what to think.' Keiva sat down on the nearest sofa with a heavy sigh. 'I treated each patient according to the diagnosis I'd come to, confident I had them covered, but who knows? They each could have had subsequent heart attacks. It happens from time to time.'

'But not five times in a row?'

'No...maybe not.'

'Campbell told me there was another one.'

Keiva met her friend's hazel gaze across the coffee-table between them. 'Yesterday.'

Lana grimaced. 'You poor darling, this must be so awful for you. How are you coping?'

'The usual way, caffeine and chocolate.'

Lana smiled softly. 'I've just boiled the kettle and I have chocolate biscuits in the pantry.'

'Lovely.' Keiva got to her feet. 'I'll help you make it.'

A few minutes later they were sitting in the bay window of the kitchen with their coffee and a plate of chocolate biscuits in front of them.

'How are you managing at home, Lana?' Keiva asked when there was a lull in the conversation. 'Is anyone coming in now to help you?'

Lana put her coffee-mug down and Keiva couldn't help noticing the slight tremble of her hand as she did so.

'Not now. I cancelled the last home help Campbell organised

for me. I want to try to do things for myself. This is the way it is and I just have to get used to it.' There was sad resignation in Lana's tone and her thin shoulders drooped as she leaned back in her wheelchair.

'It must be so hard for you,' Keiva said softly.

Lana sighed. 'You know what I miss most?'

Keiva shook her head, unable to speak for the knot of emotion tightening her throat.

'I miss being able to walk around barefoot,' Lana said. 'On hot days in the past I would wander around the garden, dipping my toes in the fishpond to cool off. Sometimes I can't quite believe I will never feel the grass of the lawn between my toes ever again.'

Keiva brushed at her eyes with the back of her hand. 'I wish I could do something to help... I feel so useless.'

'What can anyone do?' Lana said. 'My injuries are permanent.'

'Have you talked to Campbell about what you're going through?' Keiva asked.

Lana's expression clouded with pain. 'How can I talk to him when he was the one driving when the accident occurred? He feels so guilty, so torn up about what happened, that for the last two years he hasn't once mentioned that day.'

'But it wasn't his fault,' Keiva reminded her. 'It was the other driver who was drunk. It had nothing to do with Campbell's driving ability.'

'I know, dear, but you know how men are. They don't talk about their feelings and they pretend everything's all right when it isn't.'

'Do you want me to talk to him?' she offered.

Lana shook her head. 'I think he's got enough on his plate as it is. So do you, in fact. I just hope that morally corrupt journalist Ted Hurst from the *Karracullen Standard* doesn't get wind of this inquiry. Can you imagine the damage it would do to this community?'

'I've been dreading the very same thing,' Keiva admitted.

'It's hard enough as it is to attract competent medical personnel to country outposts. If a scandal erupts, it's going to be a thousand times worse.'

'It won't be all that long before your time with us is up,' Lana said. 'Have you given any more thought to what you will do once your locum here is finished?'

Keiva took another biscuit off the plate and sighed. 'I can't hide out here in the country for ever, I suppose. Tim's probably married by now. There's no point in avoiding the issue any longer.'

'Do you still love him?' Lana asked.

Keiva thought about it for a moment. Yes, she had believed herself to be in love with Timothy Perrington, had even planned to marry and have a family with him, but his idea of faithfulness had in the end not matched hers. Lucy Fairfax had been everything she was not—tall and full figured, blonde and without ambition.

'No…' She met her friend's eyes and smiled. 'I no longer feel anything for him.'

'You're only just thirty,' Lana reassured her. 'Plenty of time to settle down when the right man comes along.'

'We'll see.' She lowered her gaze as a vision of the tall, determined detective flitted into her mind, her cheeks instantly heating at the thought of his very thorough kiss the evening before.

'How is Hugh behaving himself?' Lana asked. 'Is he still intent on wooing you?'

'Hugh is under the mistaken impression that any woman between the ages of nineteen and ninety will fall at his feet if he so much as winks at them.'

Lana chuckled. 'Yes, he is rather a rake, isn't he? No wonder Evangeline left him.'

'Did you know his ex-wife?'

'Evangeline wasn't cut out for the country life,' Lana said. 'She hated the dust and the heat and flies. She stuck it out until he had some sort of fling with a junior nurse. I'm surprised she lasted as long as she did.'

'I know Hugh is a good physician but I can't help feeling uncomfortable around him,' Keiva confessed. 'And I'm not the only one.'

'You don't think...?' Lana left the sentence hanging.

Keiva felt a tiny shiver of apprehension shimmy down her spine. 'I don't know... Sometimes I think this is all a storm in a teacup but then I wonder...'

'How could someone get away with it?' Lana asked. 'Surely there would be some sort of physical evidence if each case was really murder?'

'Not always,' Keiva said. 'Traces of drugs don't always last long in the body and unless bloods are taken at or soon after death no one would be the wiser.'

'What sort of drug would induce a fatal heart attack?'

'The list is probably endless but I heard of a case once, in the States, I think, where a nurse injected potassium chloride into the patient's IV line. It causes immediate cardiac arrest.'

Lana's eyes widened. 'Have you mentioned that to the detective?'

'No.'

'Don't you think you should?' Lana asked. 'What if someone was doing exactly that? I mean, could someone have access to potassium chloride?'

'Potassium chloride is a normal salt in the human body, but in the wrong doses it can be lethal.' She gnawed at her bottom lip before adding, 'After that case came to light, a directive was sent around the country to ensure it is more closely monitored. Now all the bags have pre-added potassium. We hardly use any ampoules of potassium any more. But if someone really wanted to...' She looked at Lana once more. 'Maybe I should mention it to Detective Darcy. I didn't think of it before. Actually, to tell you the truth, I haven't been all that convinced anything untoward has happened.'

'I definitely think you should mention it to him,' Lana insisted. 'Who knows who will be next if the culprit isn't found?'

She hadn't thought of that. If what Detective Darcy suspected was true then someone else could die unless they found the perpetrator soon.

'But what I still can't imagine is why someone would kill five patients for apparently no reason,' Keiva said.

'People have all sorts of reasons for committing crimes,' Lana said. 'Maybe there's some link between all of them—you know, like in an Agatha Christie novel.'

'The only link the detective has established so far is that I treated each patient.'

'Surely he doesn't think you're responsible?'

'It's hard to know, what he really thinks,' she said. 'He hangs around the hospital so much. I can't help feeling he's watching my every move. Every time I turn a corner he seems to be there.'

'It's understandable, I suppose, that he'd want to see how things are done out here,' Lana suggested. 'He can hardly investigate the case properly if he's not on site a good deal of the time.'

Keiva's sigh communicated her reluctant agreement. 'I guess you're right.' She gave Lana a world-weary glance and added, 'He seemed to think it significant that a couple of the patients had been aggressive or verbally abusive towards me.'

'Why would that be significant?'

'I'm not sure…' Keiva frowned as she thought about Liam's line of questioning the evening before. 'Maybe someone has taken it upon themselves to protect me.'

'By killing off anyone who doesn't treat you well?' Lana's eyes were out on stalks. 'Good God, Keiva. That sounds like a Hollywood script, not something that could happen in Karracullen.'

'I know. Silly, isn't it?' Keiva smiled and got up to leave. 'Is there anything I can do for you before I head off? Shopping or something?'

Lana shook her head. 'No, thanks, Campbell will be home shortly. I have everything I need for now.'

Keiva bent down to kiss her cheek. 'Call me if you need anything. I'll try and visit you later in the week.'

'Goodbye, my dear, and thank you.'

Keiva drove past the Bullock and Dray hotel but there was no sign of Detective Darcy's car in the car park. Deciding to leave it till later, she returned to the cottage and, slipping on a bikini underneath her shorts and T-shirt, made her way out to her favourite swimming gorge.

The late morning heat was fierce but the shade offered by the cluster of eucalypts along the bank was a welcome relief as she stepped out of her clothes and slipped into the cool water.

The tension of the week seemed to dissipate as soon as the silky water flowed over her limbs, her skin tingling with delight as the heat from her body came into contact with the refreshing coolness of the deep waterhole. She began swimming towards the opposite side of the gorge, the shadows from overhanging branches shivering over the surface as she carved her way through.

The warble of magpies, the gentle slap of water over the rocky edges and the soft brush of the hot breeze were all the sounds she could hear when she finally stopped to lift her face to the sun.

She floated on her back, letting her arms drift by her sides to keep herself afloat, a deep sigh of relaxation running through her from the top of her head right down to her toes.

The startled flap of wings in the bush fringing the gorge sent her upright, her legs immediately treading water as she checked to see who had invaded her solitude.

A tall, instantly recognisable figure was standing on the rocky shelf a few feet away, his grey-blue gaze trained on her.

'How's the water?' Liam asked, with no trace of yesterday's anger in his voice.

'Wet,' she answered.

She thought she saw a glimmer of a smile pass over his face but the sun was shining in her eyes and she wondered if maybe she'd imagined it. She swam to the side where he was standing and, shading her eyes, looked up at him. 'How did you know I was here?'

'I heard this was your hide-away,' he said.

She frowned. 'Who told you that?'

'I have my sources.'

She threw him a quelling glance. 'Did you want to see me about anything in particular, or are you just here to annoy me?'

'There are a couple of things I wish to discuss with you.' He squatted down so she didn't have to crane her neck. 'I guess now's as good a time as any.'

Keiva kept back from the rocky ledge, not sure she wanted to discuss anything with him now that he'd invaded her sanctuary.

'Want a hand to get out?' He reached out his arm to her and she looked at it for a moment as if deliberating over whether to touch him or not. 'Come on, Keiva, I'm not about to arrest you. I just want to talk.' He brushed a fly away from his face with his other hand and added a touch gruffly, 'I also want to apologise for last night. I was totally out of line.'

She moved to the edge and lifted her hand to his, but as soon as his long fingers wrapped around hers some impish part of her made her tug on his hand with all her strength.

He wobbled for a moment, a look of complete shock on his handsome face before he hit the water with a startled expletive, his submerging body creating a huge splash that sent waves of water over Keiva's shaking shoulders as she began to laugh.

He surfaced right near her, his expression a combination of dented male pride and reluctant admiration for her show of spirit.

'How's the water, Detective?' she teased, still laughing.

He flipped his wet dark hair back with one hand as he looked down at her, his eyes smouldering as they locked onto hers.

She stopped laughing.

She felt the soft fluttering of desire beating its wings inside her at the undiluted male attraction she could feel coming off him in waves. Her eyes dipped to his mouth almost of their own volition, her own lips starting to tingle in remembrance of what it had felt like to have that hard male mouth against hers.

She knew he was going to kiss her but she didn't move out of reach. She realised with an almost painful jolt of awareness that she wanted him to kiss her. And not only kiss her. She wanted him to take her in his arms and make her feel like a desirable woman, make her forget about her disastrous relationship with Tim. Make her feel as powerfully feminine as a woman could feel in the arms of a man who burned with desire for her, only her.

Liam's mouth came down on hers roughly at first, almost savagely, as if he could barely control his response to her. Keiva kissed him back, nipping at his bottom lip with teasing little bites that only served to incite him more. She heard the low growl at the back of his throat as his arms came around her, his long legs entwining with hers beneath the water. Even though he was still wearing jeans and a T-shirt, she could feel every ridge and plane of his body, the wet rough fabric of his clothes doing little to disguise his potent arousal.

Keiva barely knew him but she wanted him with a passion she hadn't thought possible.

When one of his hands came over her breast she gasped at the feel of his broad thumb against her jutting nipple as he teased her bikini top to one side. She felt the scorch of his gaze as he looked down at her exposed flesh where the pad of his thumb was rolling back and forth in lazy sensual strokes.

His mouth returned to hers with increasing heat, his tongue circling hers in a dance of growing desire she could feel pulsating from his body into hers.

Without thinking of the consequences, she reached for the waistband of his jeans and lowered the zipper, her fingers searching for him as their entwined legs struggled to keep them afloat.

Liam tore his mouth off hers to look down at her, his eyes glittering with unrelieved need. 'I don't think that's such a good idea right now.'

Disappointment washed over her, as well as a good measure of shame at her uncharacteristic wantonness.

'You don't?'

He reached out and touched her face, his small smile wry. 'Putting a condom on is awkward at the best of times, and even if I had one on me, in ten feet of water I'd say it was just about impossible.'

She couldn't help admiring his reasoning, a part of her pleased he was responsible enough to consider her safety as well as his. She tilted her head at him, injecting her tone with a playful note, even though inside she felt the full weight of shame at her forwardness. 'Maybe some other time?'

He kissed her once, firmly. 'Definitely some other time.'

She made her way to the ledge and lifted herself out, standing to watch as he did the same. She couldn't take her eyes off the bulging of his arm muscles as he vaulted out of the water, the line of his tall body fit and strong.

She reached for her things to disguise her reaction to him, hoping he would put her heightened colour down to the effort of getting out of the water instead of what had occurred within it. She slipped on her shorts and T-shirt over her wet bikini and finger-combed her hair before turning back to face him. 'I'm sorry, I don't have a spare towel. Do you want to borrow mine?'

He took it from her and gave his hair a rough wipe before handing it back to her. 'I'll be fine, it's hot. I'll be dry in no time.'

She draped the towel over her shoulder, sure she could smell the fragrance of his hair clinging to the fabric, making her feel as if they had just passed some sort of intimate barrier.

She looked at him, hunting his face for some indication of

what he was feeling, but his expression gave nothing away. She realised she should probably apologise and began to stumble through it awkwardly. 'I shouldn't have pulled you in like that. It was…childish of me… I'm sorry…'

'I think we're more or less square,' he said. 'I shouldn't have kissed you last night. It was unprofessional.'

She really wanted to argue with him on that point. His kiss had been very professional, as far as she was concerned!

'What about just now?' she asked. 'Was that unprofessional, too?'

'That was different.'

'How so?'

'I wasn't here on business.'

'Why were you here?' she asked.

'I wanted to see you.'

'Why?'

He seemed reluctant to answer. She watched as he hunted for his keys in his jeans pocket, his face turned away from her probing gaze.

'Liam?' His name slipped off her tongue as she touched him on the arm.

He turned to look at her, his eyes going to where her fingers lay against his skin. He placed his hand over hers and tugged her towards him. 'You know what, Dr Truscott?' he asked, holding her intent gaze. 'You ask too many damn questions.' And then he covered her mouth with his.

CHAPTER SEVEN

THIS time Liam's kiss was gentler, as if he wanted to take his time exploring every nuance of her mouth, committing it to his memory so he could take it out and re-examine it at his leisure. Keiva gave a soft sigh against the persuasive pressure of his lips, her stomach free-falling when he probed his tongue through the seam of her mouth. He tasted so damn good, so male and minty, so in control as he held her along the pulsing heat of his hard body.

After a breathless minute or two he lifted his mouth from hers and looked down at her upturned face, the pad of his thumb rolling over the swollen curve of her bottom lip just as it had done with her breast a few minutes before.

'I don't suppose there's anywhere in Karracullen where we could have dinner together tonight without causing a wave of gossip, is there?' he asked.

She smiled a little shyly. 'No…but you could come to my place if you like. I can cook…well, sort of.'

'To tell you the truth, I'm not all that worried about food.' He pressed another sensual kiss to her mouth.

'So, do we have a date, Dr Truscott?' he asked, his direct gaze glinting with desire.

'We certainly do,' she said, and pulled his head back down to hers.

Keiva drove back to town a short while later very conscious of Liam following her. She kept glancing in her rear-view mirror, unable to quell her tiny shiver of delight every time she saw him behind her. His eyes were masked by the sunglasses he was wearing, but she could see the line of his mouth, the way it was softened by a small smile every time her glance fell

81

his way. She took the turn-off to her street and watched as he drove past, lifting his hand in a single wave before the dust stirred up by his tyres gradually made him disappear from view.

It was only later, as she was agonising over what to wear that evening, that the doubts began to surface, floating around her consciousness until she could no longer ignore them. Her response to Liam both shocked and delighted her. For months she'd considered herself to be one of those unfortunate women who had little or no libido, putting down the collapse of her relationship to Tim to exactly that reason—lack of physical desire. It had helped her to understand why he had sought the arms of Lucy Fairfax, not necessarily excusing his unfaithfulness but coming to a place inside herself where she could gradually let it go as one of those things that had been more or less inevitable. However, her behaviour in the arms of Liam made her realise that it wasn't desire she lacked, but rather a measure of self-control. How could she have agreed to take their relationship that one step further? She cringed as she thought about how she had clawed at his wet clothing like some sex-starved country girl who hadn't seen a bit of male flesh in months. What must he think of her? She was a doctor, for heaven's sake! She had to uphold some sort of moral responsibility. It more or less went with the territory of being the caretaker of other people's health.

It shocked and shamed her that she had been prepared to risk either pregnancy or disease out there at the gorge, never once stopping to think about protection. Was that what she had been missing with Tim? The overwhelming rush of fiery need that caused a storm in the blood, flowing tumultuously over every firm principle until nothing was left but exultant feeling?

The only trouble was what to do now that rationality had returned. Keiva glanced at her watch and a ragged sigh escaped her lips. She had less than five hours to find something to wear, organise something to cook and have a damn good reason ready for why she didn't think it wise for them to sleep together. Liam was here for a short space of time while he conducted his inquiry. Within weeks he would be gone, leaving her with the memories of an affair that could never promise longevity. How could she consent to such an arrangement? There was nothing in her personality that bent towards the casual. It had taken months before Tim had convinced her to agree to marry him, even longer to get her into his bed.

Liam had grilled her with questions, looked at her narrow-eyed with suspicion and yet she had been ready to lie down on the rocks at the gorge to accept him. Was there something terribly wrong with her?

She stared at her phone, trying to think of an adequate excuse for calling off their date, her fingers hovering over the keypad in indecision. When it rang in her hand, she nearly dropped it in surprise.

'H-hello?'

'Keiva.' It was Grace Connor, the nursing supervisor. 'Sorry to land this on you at short notice, but Ryan Morris just called in sick. He's got that stomach virus that's been going round. Can you do his shift this evening? I've asked Dr Portland but it's his wedding anniversary. He said he would do it but only if you couldn't.'

Keiva chewed her lip for a moment. 'All right.' She gave an inward sigh. Here was the out she'd been looking for, but now it was here she wasn't all that sure she wanted to take it.

'Thanks, Keiva.' Grace cut across her private rumination. 'I told John you'd be the one to do it. I think he was scared Susanne would leave him if he didn't keep this evening free. You know how she can be at times.'

'No problem,' Keiva answered. 'I've got nothing better to do.'

'No hot date tonight?' Grace asked. 'I thought I heard you and the detective were spending a bit of time together.'

'What is it with this town?' Keiva asked with more than a

hint of asperity to her tone. 'I hardly know the man and everybody already has me in his bed.'

'If I were twenty years younger, my girl, I'd be fighting you for the right-hand side.'

Keiva put the phone down a short time later and shook her head as she reached for her keys. 'Who needs a bed?' she asked the silence of her cottage kitchen.

The gorge would have done just fine.

Liam was in the supermarket deciding which box of chocolates to buy for Keiva when his mobile phone bleeped, indicating an incoming text message. He glanced down at it and frowned.

He put the chocolates back and made his way to the cashier, adding a few inconsequential items to his basket on his way, lifting it so the girl at the register could tally the total.

Cassie King gave him a bright smile. 'Hello, Detective, have you got a busy evening planned?'

He wasn't sure how to answer. He'd planned a very busy evening indeed, showing Keiva how much she turned him on, but it seemed a rain-check had been instigated. It was hard to know from the brief wording of her text message if she was pulling out of their date due to having second thoughts about getting involved with him or whether a genuine emergency had occurred.

He sighed as he handed over the money, 'No, nothing special planned.'

Cassie handed the bag of groceries over the counter. 'You doing anything tomorrow?' she asked.

He didn't answer immediately and she blushed delicately and raced on, 'I know you're probably busy but, seeing you're from the city, I thought you might be interested in coming to the Karracullen rodeo. It's on tomorrow out at the showground.'

'That sounds interesting.'

Her young face gleamed. 'I'm riding in the barrel race. I've won it for the last three years.'

Liam smiled. 'Then I'd better not miss it. What time does it start?'

Cassie's eyes almost popped out of her head. 'You mean you'll come? *Really?*'

He gave a loose shrug. 'Why not? Sounds like fun.'

'Oh, it is!' The young girl was in raptures. 'It's the best fun. It starts at ten and rocks on until late.'

'I'll be there with spurs on.' He flashed her yet another smile and made his way to the exit.

'Jamie Sweeney's just arrived, Keiva,' Nicole Fordham, the nurse on duty, informed her as she arrived in A and E. 'His parents just brought him in. He's got a very bad fracture of his right femur. Could be compound.'

Keiva went straight to where the young lad was lying on a trolley, groaning in pain. His parents were beside him, looking absolutely stricken.

'Jamie, can you tell me what happened?'

'I fell off a rope…at the dam…' He gave a rough sob.

'He was swinging into the water from a tyre swing at the gorge out past the Hendersons' place,' Jamie's father said. 'The rope broke and he fell on the rocks. His leg was so badly bent we got him in the car and brought him straight in. He's in so much pain…can you do something for him?'

'Of course.' Keiva sent the parents a reassuring glance. 'Why don't you two wait outside while we sort Jamie out? We need some room to move in here, and as soon as we know the extent of his injury I'll send someone out to inform you.'

She turned to Nicole once Jamie's parents had left. 'Nic, get in a cannula and give 10 milligrams morphine IV straight off, and start one litre of normal saline to run in, stat. There'll be significant blood loss into that fracture site.'

'His foot is blue,' Nicole pointed out.

'Right, get the resident on duty in here and get a Donway splint. The right femur's badly angulated and it's either cut off the blood supply or we've got a vascular injury. Either way, this is going to need Theatre. Call in Geoffrey Ellerton and warn Theatre.'

Peter Frost, the junior resident, came in with the splint. 'I might need some help with this,' he said. 'I've never actually put on one before.'

'You'll learn once you do the EMST course, Peter,' Keiva said. 'Here, slide the splint up to the groin while I straighten the leg as gently as possible. Hopefully that morphine has taken the edge off. Jamie, I'm going to have to straighten your leg. The bend is cutting off the blood flow and I can't feel any pulses in your foot. It'll hurt but we have to do it now.'

Keiva put traction on the right lower limb, straightening out the whole leg. Jamie screamed in pain but she held the leg straight while Peter put the splint in place, then she attached the foot to the foot-plate and began to pump up the splint, which straightened the leg even further.

'Sorry, mate.' Keiva addressed Jamie with an apologetic grimace. 'But we had to get that leg straightened. I can feel peripheral pulses in the foot now. We'll give you some more pain relief.' She flicked a glance Nicole's way. 'Another 5 milligrams morphine IV, Nic. What's his pulse and BP?'

'Pulse 120, BP 120 over 80. There's bleeding coming from that wound on the thigh,' Nicole said.

'Yes, it's a compound fracture. It's going to need nailing and antibiotics. When did you last eat or drink, Jamie?'

'I had something at three o'clock,' he gulped on a sob of pain. 'A drink and a chocolate bar.'

Keiva couldn't help thinking she could do with a chocolate bar right now, maybe even two.

'Theatre just told me they'll be ready in half an hour,' Nicole said as she came back from the telephone. 'And here's the anaesthetic registrar now.'

Keiva looked up as Carol came in. 'He's fasted for over four hours, Carol. We've got crystalloid pouring in and BP's OK. We've cross-matched four units and bloods have been taken.

ECG is OK. Sats are OK on the mask. He's right to transport to Theatre when you're ready.'

'The orderly is on his way,' Carol said, looking down at the patient. 'You don't look so good.'

'You should feel it from my side,' Jamie groaned.

Keiva exchanged glances with Nicole as Jamie was wheeled out of A and E. 'Is it my turn to meet the parents?'

'You're the doctor.' Nicole stripped off her gloves. 'The buck stops with you, right?'

Keiva shouldered open the door, her expression rueful. 'Tell me again why I decided to be an A and E doctor.'

Nicole laughed. 'You love people, you're a workaholic and you don't have a social life.'

'That just about sums it up,' Keiva agreed as she left.

Keiva made her way out to the showground the next morning, having promised to be a medical presence as back up to the paramedic team in case of an emergency.

She carried her doctor's bag to the steward's office and, leaving it there, made her way to the Country Women's Association tent in search of a cup of tea.

'Keiva!' Mavis Poppy bustled over to her with a plate of scones piled high with jam and cream. 'Sit yourself down and I'll get you a cuppa. How are things at the hospital? And how's that dishy detective, eh?'

Keiva gave her a wan smile and bit into a scone to avoid answering. 'Mmm…' She licked up an escaping dollop of rich country cream. 'Delicious.'

'I thought so, too.' Mavis grinned. 'So tall! And those piercing eyes.'

Keiva felt her face flame as she realised what she'd inadvertently said. Mavis was like the Karracullen telephone exchange—if she heard a bit of gossip, everybody heard it.

'I meant the cream and jam.' She pointed to the scone in her hand.

Mavis thrust her hands on her generous hips and rolled her eyes. 'Sure you did.'

She tried another tack. 'How's your leg doing?'

It was a stroke of genius, Keiva thought ten minutes later when the elderly woman still hadn't drawn breath on the ongoing saga of her leg ulcers. It was only the arrival of Campbell, pushing Lana's chair into the tent, that interrupted the process. Keiva smiled warmly and with considerable relief as they came to share her trestle table.

'I heard you were rostered on today,' Campbell said, reaching for a scone. 'Ever been to a rodeo before?'

She shook her head. 'No, this is my first. I'm not all that sure I agree ideologically with the riding of protesting animals. Do they get hurt?'

'The ones to get hurt are usually the cowboys.' Campbell's expression was wry.

'I'm inclined to agree with you, Keiva,' Lana said as she stirred her cup of tea. 'I don't like the thought of roping calves and throwing them to the ground just for the hell of it.'

'It's sport,' Campbell protested, reaching for another scone. 'What else is there to do out here? Look at those young lads over there. They can't wait to test their strength and ability. Better to do it on a wild bull's back than hold up the local bank or store just for fun.'

'Maybe…' Keiva twirled her teaspoon thoughtfully.

'Uh-oh,' Campbell warned in an undertone. 'Look who's on the prowl. Mr Gossip himself, Ted Hurst.'

Keiva turned her head to see the *Karracullen Standard* journalist making a beeline for their table.

'Am I interrupting anything?' he asked as he swung a leg over the bench seat.

'Not at all.' Keiva gave him what she hoped was a polite smile. 'How are you, Ted?'

'All the better for seeing you.' He grinned wolfishly and reached for the last scone. 'I heard you're the linchpin of a murder inquiry. Want to give me the full story?'

'There's no story,' she said, flicking Campbell a worried glance. 'So far it's just a review of some cases.'

'Some suspicious cases,' Ted mused. 'Word has it the detective is close to nailing the culprit.'

Keiva pursed her lips in an effort to stop herself from responding. She knew what Ted Hurst was like. He would stop at nothing for a front-page story, even making it up if he had to.

'Come on, Ted,' Campbell interjected. 'Don't go making a headline out of nothing. Five or six people had fatal heart attacks. So what? Do you know how many people across the country have had heart attacks while we've been sitting here? Heart disease is the number one killer, even more than traffic accidents or any type of cancer. You'd be better to run a story on how people can get off their backsides and exercise—that would actually do some good instead of stirring up a hornet's nest for no reason.'

'The community of Karracullen has the right to know what's been going on,' Ted insisted. 'If there's an issue of malpractice by a medical practitioner, it needs to be made public.'

'If that's the case, the detective will do what has to be done. There are proper channels for this sort of thing. It doesn't help the process with a whole lot of innuendo and speculation from outsiders,' Keiva said.

'If you ask me, I think it's a ridiculous waste of time,' Campbell said. 'Liam Darcy seems a genuine enough fellow, but if he's looking for a fast track to promotion this isn't going to do it. There's absolutely no evidence to suggest foul play, and without evidence there is no case for prosecution.'

Mavis reappeared at that point with another plate of scones, and Keiva rose from the table, making her excuses so she could escape before she had to sit through another recounting of the older woman's medical history.

She was on her way to the grandstand when she saw Liam talking to one of the local farmers. She stayed in the shadow of the building so she could watch him undisturbed, hoping the milling crowd would think she was simply keeping out of the sun instead of feasting her eyes on the handsome detective.

He was wearing moleskins, which made him look right at home amongst the locals, his blue open-necked shirt highlighting the colour of his eyes and the breadth of his chest. He was smiling at the farmer, his teeth white against his tan, his expression open and friendly.

The farmer moved away and Liam suddenly turned to look at her. Keiva felt like a child who'd been caught with their hand in the cookie jar and swung around, fast-tracking it to the front of the grandstand where the first event was about to start.

The smell of horse sweat, hay and dust was thick in the air as she leaned against the rail, pretending an interest she really didn't feel as the first rodeo rider took his place in the chute, waiting for his moment to mount the thrashing brumby.

The gates burst open with a clang of metal and the roar of the crowd, the dust rising in thick clouds as the agitated horse's hooves bit at the ground in an effort to dislodge the rider, who was hanging on determinedly, his hat flying off to land in the churned-up soil.

Keiva held her breath, her mind racing with possible scenarios of injury if the horse managed to dislodge its rider. The flying hooves made her visibly wince. She could imagine the damage they could do if they were to land on the flesh of the abdomen or, even worse, the rider's unprotected head.

The crowd roared as the rider made the time limit, jumping off with a victorious lift of his hand.

She sensed rather than saw Liam come to stand beside her at the protective railing. All the fine hairs on the back of her neck lifted like antennae, her skin tingled and her mouth went suddenly dry.

'Sorry about last night.' She gave him an apologetic look. 'Duty called, I'm afraid.'

He didn't answer immediately and she wondered if he thought she'd pulled the plug on last night deliberately. She could see the scepticism in his eyes as they meshed with hers, and the way one corner of his mouth was tilted just a fraction.

'You can check the hospital records if you don't believe me,' she said tightly.

His eyes dipped to her mouth and lingered there for a heart-beat before returning to the action being played out in the arena in front of them. 'Looks like fun,' he said, his deep voice stroking her like a sensual caress.

'Not for the horse,' she returned, giving him a quick side-ways glance.

He leaned against the rail with his forearms, his gaze when it slanted her way on a level with hers. This close she could see the tiny flecks of grey in his eyes. When she glanced down to where his arm rested so near hers she saw the masculine sun-bronzed hairs on his arm almost touching her exposed skin.

He looked back at the action in the riding yard, narrowing his eyes against the sun. 'It looks dangerous for both horse and rider.' He shifted his glance back to her. 'Is that why you're here, in a professional capacity?'

She nodded. 'I left my doctor's bag in the stewards' room. There's a paramedic team over there.' She pointed to the left of the grandstand where an ambulance was parked in the shade of a group of peppercorn trees. 'But if things get nasty it's always good to have a spare pair of hands. I've been trained in the early management of severe trauma.'

'EMST for short, right?'

'That's right,' she answered. 'Rural doctors need that sort of skill out here. It can literally be the difference between life and death.'

Keiva looked at the next horse as it exploded into the yard, the rider almost losing his balance as it reared and bucked violently beneath him. When the rider fell before the time limit was up, he got up and shook himself off, scooping up his hat on the way back to the safety fence as the crowd gave him an encouraging cheer.

Keiva felt Liam readjust his position beside her, his forearm touching hers briefly, hotly and tantalisingly.

'This thing we have going on between us…' He turned to look at her, his expression hard to read on account of the bright sunlight. 'I think we should be honest from the outset, you know, lay down some ground rules.'

She took an unsteady breath and lowered her gaze a fraction. 'What happened out at the gorge shouldn't have happened. You caught me off guard and I…I reacted without thinking.' She bit her lip and added, 'Even if I hadn't been called in last night, I'm not sure I would have…you know… I'm not a casual sex person…I never have been. I'm sorry, I shouldn't have led you on like that. It was…'

'Unprofessional?' His eyes drew hers back to his.

'Out of character,' she amended, looking away again.

He turned back to look at the activity in the arena as another wild brumby burst from the gates, the rider barely managing to ride out the first few humping bucks.

The crowd gave a collective indrawn gasp as he began to tilt to one side, one of his legs failing to come out of the stirrup as he slipped even further, to hang in an ungainly fashion beneath the horse's stomach. The wild hooves created a dusty blur as they struck him repeatedly in the chest and torso as he was dragged along the ground.

'Quick!' Keiva turned her head to Liam as she began to climb the safety rail. 'Can you get my bag for me? It's in the stewards' room next to the CWA tent. I'd better get started down here.'

She was over the fence and into the yard just as the control riders secured the brumby, one of the men releasing the rider's caught leg.

The crowd was ominously silent behind her as Keiva bent down to check for breathing and pulse in the crumpled and now eerily still body lying in the dust…

CHAPTER EIGHT

LIAM arrived with her bag just as the ambulance team unfolded the trolley to move the man out of the ring.

'Don't move him yet!' Keiva said quickly.

'Dr Truscott.' The most senior ambulance officer addressed her. 'We need to get him to hospital quickly. He's in shock. We can't do much for him here.'

'Listen, Dave, isn't it?' She recognised him from one of his previous drop-offs. 'We need to stabilise him a bit before we move him. He's probably got a neck injury. Have you got a hard cervical collar?'

'Yes, in the kit. What size?'

'Looks like a medium.' She turned to the other officer. 'Bob, hold his head still while I fit the collar. Good. Now, listen, guys, you've got oxygen—let's get a mask on and high flow. Can I have those gloves and goggles, Dave?'

'Sure. Should we get him moved now?'

'Not yet. His airway is clear, he's unconscious and not responding to voice or pain, but his breathing is shallow and rapid. Unless we treat that here, he'll be dead before you get out of the arena.'

Keiva listened to the patient's chest with the stethoscope from her emergency kit, then percussed his chest and felt for the position of the trachea. The rider's shirt had been ripped off in places, and there was clearly marked bruising and bony crepitus over the right side of his chest, as well as surgical emphysema.

'He has a right tension pneumothorax. If we don't fix that now he'll die in minutes. Give me two of the largest IV cannulas you've got, Dave.'

Dave rooted around in the ambulance medical kit, produced

93

two 14-gauge IV needles and handed them to her. She carefully inserted both of them into the second intercostal space in the mid-clavicular line on the right, producing a hiss of escaping air and obvious improvement in the depth of the patient's respiratory excursion.

'That will hold him until we get to Emergency. We can radio ahead and set up for a proper chest drain as soon as he arrives. Hand me your BP cuff, Bob.'

He obliged, looking relieved that some semblance of control was being gained by one very cool and competent woman.

'Pulse is 120 and thready, BP 70 systolic, hands are cold and clammy. He's in severe shock, presumably hypovolaemic. His abdomen is bruised on the right, too. My guess is he has a liver injury with intra-abdominal bleeding. He won't last long unless we get some volume on board. Are you guys carrying IV fluids?'

'Yeah, we've got normal saline and giving sets,' replied Dave, pulling them from the ambulance's kit.

Keiva took another 14 gauge IV cannula and inserted it into a right arm vein.

'Pump in this saline as quickly as you can, Bob. Now, let's get your spine board and get things moving. We'll need a couple of helpers to log roll him onto the spine board.'

Liam stepped forward and she gave him a quick grateful glance.

'I'll control the neck. On my count…one…two…three.'

Under Keiva's careful direction and control, the severely injured rider was stabilised and packaged for transport to A and E. Keiva rode along in the back of the ambulance, controlling the rider's neck and airway, while Bob pumped in IV fluid and Dave drove at a fast but safe rate to the hospital, radioing ahead with details of their patient and treatment.

On arrival at the hospital Geoffrey took control with his surgical team at the ready.

'Good work, Keiva,' he said as the trolley was wheeled through to Theatre. 'Just as well you were out there. This looks bad but it could have been a whole lot worse. I'll see what I can do and fill you in later.'

Keiva gave him a wan smile as she peeled off her gloves, dropping them in the nearest bin as the theatre doors swung shut behind the senior surgeon.

She turned to find Liam standing, waiting for her, his mole-skins and blue shirt not much cleaner than her own gear, which was covered in thick dust and blood.

'You look terrible,' he said, running his gaze over her.

'Thanks.' Her mouth twisted.

'You were amazing out there.'

'So were you.' She gave him a small smile. 'Thanks for getting my bag for me.'

'I thought I'd better come to town to take you back to your car.'

She looked down at herself and grimaced. 'I should get changed first.'

'Come on, then.' He jangled his keys and led the way. 'We'll go via your place.'

Keiva fell into step beside him, inordinately pleased he'd come to fetch her. It seemed to her to indicate he hadn't been offended by her earlier announcement about their relationship, but had taken it in his stride with ease. She chanced a glance at him while he was driving, wondering what was going on behind the screen of his eyes as they squinted against the afternoon sunlight.

Liam turned and caught her looking at him, his mouth tilting in a lopsided smile. 'You've got dust on the end of your nose.'

She lifted a hand and found it to be true. 'I can even feel it between my teeth. That poor guy is going to have a job fighting infection with it all through his wounds.'

'Just as long as he doesn't have a heart attack,' he commented, turning back to the road ahead.

Keiva frowned, looking his way once more. 'You surely don't think someone would…?'

He turned the corner into her street and parked his car outside her house before he turned to look at her, his expression serious. 'Keiva, I know you don't like admitting the possibility, but the more I think about this case the more I suspect it's likely to happen again. Mr Holt's death was a little too coincidental.'

'Mr Holt's death was well within the bounds of normal for a man of his age and state of health,' she insisted, still unwilling to think about other explanations.

'Maybe.' He killed the engine. 'But until I can be sure I want you to be on the constant lookout for anything.. and I mean *anything*—unusual.'

She stared at him in a combination of alarm and confusion. 'I thought you hadn't yet ruled me out? Isn't that why you follow me like a shadow all the time?'

He gave her a studied look, his eyes holding hers for endless seconds. 'Go and get changed. I'll wait for you out here.'

A few minutes later she came back out to his car dressed in a pair of jeans and fresh crop top, the heat from the sun already causing fine droplets of moisture to bead between her breasts and shoulder blades.

Liam was leaning against the bonnet of the car, talking into his mobile phone. He glanced at her briefly as she approached and then, terminating the call, pocketed the phone and opened her door.

'Thanks,' she said as she slipped into the cool interior and fastened her seat belt, wondering what had brought about that heavy frown to settle between his eyes.

He got into the driver's side and gunned the engine, backing out of the space with the sort of understated competence she couldn't help admiring. Tim had always driven erratically and aggressively, nudging his way through traffic as if he had permanent right of way. It amazed her to think how close she had been to committing her life to him. How could she have got it so wrong?

Play The *Lucky Hearts* Game

and get...

FREE BOOKS & a FREE GIFT...

YOURS to KEEP!

Yes! I have scratched off the silver card. Please send me my **FREE BOOKS** and **FREE MYSTERY GIFT**. I understand that I am under no obligation to purchase any books as explained on the back of this card. I am over 18 years of age.

Scratch Here!
then look below to see
what you can claim...

M5II

Mrs/Miss/Ms/Mr _____ Initials _____

BLOCK CAPITALS PLEASE

Surname _____

Address _____

_____

_____

Postcode _____

Twenty-one gets you
4 FREE BOOKS and a
MYSTERY GIFT!

Twenty gets you
1 FREE BOOK and a
MYSTERY GIFT!

Nineteen gets you
1 FREE BOOK!

TRY AGAIN!

The Reader Service™ — Here's how it works:

THE READER SERVICE™
FREE BOOK OFFER
FREEPOST CN81
CROYDON
CR9 3WZ

NO STAMP
NECESSARY
IF POSTED IN
THE U.K. OR N.I.

Cassie King bounded up to them both as they walked past the grandstand a few minutes later.

'Dr Truscott! Detective Darcy! My race is on in ten minutes—will you come and watch?'

Liam glanced at Keiva. 'How about it, Doctor? Shall we go and watch this young lady whip the backsides of the opposition?'

Keiva smiled at the young girl. 'I wouldn't miss it for the world, but only if you promise not to fall off, break bones or injure the horse.'

Cassie looked aghast at the suggestion. 'Hurt Sylvaner? I'd rather die myself than hurt him.'

She bounced off to get ready, her freckled face gleaming with anticipated victory.

'I hope she's going to be all right,' Keiva couldn't help saying as they found a seat in the grandstand.

'She'll be fine,' Liam reassured her. 'I was talking to her father earlier. That kid was practically born in the saddle. It will take a lot to shift her out of it, or so Paddy King says.'

Keiva forced her shoulders to relax, but after the earlier drama her adrenalin levels were still high, making her edgy and ill at ease.

'Look, here she comes,' she said as Cassie entered the arena in the distance.

Liam followed her line of vision. 'The competition looks stiff,' he observed. 'She's the youngest by far.'

Within minutes the first couple of contestants had ridden in a cloverleaf pattern around the three barrels, the judge adding five seconds to their times for every barrel they knocked over. The first rider managed to get through the course without knocking any barrels over but the second and third each knocked over two apiece. Another three contestants went through the course with slightly better results, two having clear rounds and the third only knocking over one barrel.

Finally it was Cassie's turn. Her Palomino horse was prancing at the start, eager to run the course, his nostrils flaring in excitement, his hooves stirring the dust in great billowing clouds.

The steward lifted his flag and off Cassie went, her tiny frame clinging like a second skin to the powerful back and shoulders of her horse. Sylvaner moved so quickly the dust obscured most of the action of his feet, but it was clear from the victorious shouts from the King family end of the stand that once again Cassie had beaten the opposition with not only a clear round but the fastest time overall.

Keiva clapped her hands as the young girl was presented with her trophy, lifting it high in the air, her young face gleaming with achievement as she sought her family and friends in the crowd. Keiva waved at her and then turned to Liam, her eyes shining with delight. 'Wasn't she wonderful?'

Liam gave her a somewhat distracted smile and got to his feet. 'Will you excuse me? I have to check on something.'

She frowned and twisted in her seat to see where he was going, but he wove his way through the crowd to the other side of the grandstand, taking the steps down two at a time until he disappeared from view.

'Hi, Keiva.' Jane sank into the seat beside her, fanning her hot face with a programme. 'Hot, isn't it?'

Keiva turned and smiled. 'Sure is. Have you just got here?'

Jane nodded. 'Billy's in the steer-roping in a few minutes. I heard about Brandon Clete's fall. Do you think he's going to be all right?'

'I'm not sure. Geoffrey's dealing with it as we speak. He certainly copped a fair beating.'

'These guys are tough.' Jane spoke with the confidence of someone who had spent her entire lifetime in the country. 'Billy's had a few nasty tumbles but still comes back for more. It's what cowboys do.'

'Remind me never to get involved with a cowboy.' Keiva gave an inward shudder.

'What about getting involved with a detective?' Jane gave her a probing look.

Keiva kept her line of vision trained straight ahead. 'I don't think so.'

'Come on, Keiva, the guy's gorgeous. I heard he was around at your place the other night.'

Keiva turned sharply to look at her. 'Who told you that?'

'You don't exactly live on an empty street,' Jane pointed out wryly. 'You've got at least six neighbours, two of which are the mainstay of Karracullen's gossip hotline. What they don't hear and see didn't happen as far as this community is concerned.'

'So he interviewed me at home, so what?' She turned back to face the arena.

'Is he any closer to a finding on the deaths?' Jane asked.

'I don't know... I think he wants to order an autopsy on Mr Holt.'

Jane let her breath out through the screen of her teeth. 'What's your feeling on this? Do you think someone could have induced a heart attack in each case?'

Keiva frowned and turned back to face her. 'Do you remember hearing about that case in the States where a nurse injected potassium chloride into several patients' IV lines?'

Jane's eyes widened as she recalled the incident they'd discussed some months ago in the staff tearoom. 'You think that happened *here*? At Karracullen Base?'

'I don't know what to think,' she confessed. 'It sounds like something from one of those crime shows, not something that can happen to real people, but now I'm not so sure.'

Jane's forehead furrowed. 'You know, even though they've been gradually been phased out for better control, there are always some vials of potassium on the IV trolley for patients who need extra. It wouldn't be all that difficult to siphon some off when no one was looking.'

Keiva looked at her. 'But who would do something like that, and why? Come on, Jane, we're talking about our colleagues and friends here. This is not some large impersonal hospital where no one knows who's operating the next shift.'

'I see what you mean...' Jane chewed her lip thoughtfully.

'The other pertinent point is that unless the perpetrator is caught in the act, there's practically no way of laying charges.'

Jane gave her a worried look. 'You mean they could do it again and get away with it?'

Keiva nodded grimly. 'Scary, isn't it?'

The clang of the metal gates being thrust back interrupted their conversation as Jane's husband came bursting through the shoot to rope the first steer.

Keiva watched with bated breath as Billy rode his horse alongside the running steer, skilfully roping one of its horns before turning to race back behind it so it tripped over the rope. While the animal was down he leapt off his mount and quickly tied the steer's hind legs together to the roar of the admiring crowd.

'Isn't he fabulous?' Jane's face shone with pride.

Keiva didn't think it was quite the right time to tell her friend and colleague her sympathy lay with the steer. Instead, she gave her an answering smile and agreed. 'Yes, he sure is.'

Once the main events were over in the arena, a barbeque was held in the shade of the peppercorn trees, with a bush dance accompanied by the local country and western band to finish off.

Keiva hadn't intended staying on but before she could escape someone had thrust a paper plate in her direction and the delicious smell of frying onions in the air made refusing virtually impossible.

Mavis was in her element, filling up everyone's plates with a selection of salad and thick chunks of bread to go with the man-sized steaks the men were preparing on the large barbeque.

'Here you are.' She dolloped some coleslaw on Keiva's plate. 'Where's that nice detective of yours? Chasing another suspect?'

Keiva was intensely aware of the interested glances from the people gathered around waiting for their meals. As far as she knew, the general community hadn't been informed of the real reason for Detective Darcy's visit. It made her uneasy to think of someone doing so without a thought to the consequences.

'I have no idea where he might be,' she answered, as evenly as she could.

One of the men stepped out of the meat queue to approach and she saw it was Paddy King, Cassie's father.

'Is it true, Dr Truscott?' he asked, his weatherbeaten face deeply etched in a frown. 'Ted Hurst is saying there's some trouble at the hospital, something about suspicious deaths.'

'There's really nothing to worry about.' She tried to make her voice sound as calm as possible, even though she felt her insides shrinking in alarm at how quickly the news had spread. 'The detective is here to make a few enquiries, that's all.'

There was a murmur through the gathered crowd and Keiva's heart sank at the thought of how far and wide the gossip would spread by morning.

'Here's the detective now,' Mavis said, reaching for a plate to hand to him. 'Here you go, Detective Darcy.' She smiled at him girlishly. 'Come and help yourself to a good country meal.'

'Thank you.' Liam smiled back, his gaze flicking briefly towards Keiva's troubled eyes.

'Everyone's saying there's been a murder at the hospital.' Paddy came to stand in front of him. 'Is it true?'

Keiva met Liam's speculative gaze with a they-didn't-hear-it-from-me look.

Liam looked at the farmer, his expression polite but cool. 'I haven't as yet established anything of that nature. But if and when I do, the people of Karracullen will be informed through the appropriate channels.'

'But what if it's true?' another member of the crowd asked. 'Who's going to be next to get the chop while you're still investigating?'

'I'm sure there's really nothing to worry about,' Liam assured him calmly.

'How come the local cops aren't doing the investigation?' Paddy asked. 'Colin Drummond is sharp as a tack. He ought to be able to sort things out.'

'The investigation at this stage is still an external matter,' Liam informed him. 'I've met with Commander Drummond as well as the two constables, and they are helping me with my enquiries where possible. But so far there is really nothing to report.'

'I bet it's one of the nurses,' a woman in the group said to the person standing next to her. 'I never liked that one with the red hair—what was her name again?'

'I know the one you mean,' Mavis piped up. 'She was positively cruel when I was in for my leg. Did I tell you what she said when I asked for more pain relief?'

Keiva drew in a frustrated breath and moved away, unwilling to hear another word in case she lost her temper completely.

Liam caught up with her a few moments later as she sat on a bench some distance from the food tables.

'I take it the gossip network is hot and running?'

She sighed and made room for him on the bench. 'It's only a matter of time before my name comes up, and then my career will be over.'

'That's not necessarily true.'

'Isn't it?' She gave him a sharp glance.

'I wouldn't be too worried if I were you,' he said. 'I'm hoping to wrap this up before anyone's reputation is damaged.'

She got to her feet and faced him, her expression grim. 'Easy for you to say, you stand to gain from this inquiry. You seem to forget that, whatever the outcome of this, my name is going to be permanently linked to this investigation. It really doesn't matter what the final outcome is, people are still going to have their own biased opinions.'

'You worry too much,' he said.

'No, Detective Darcy, you're wrong. The fact is I've *seen*

too much. I've been down this road before with my father. I can't go down it again. I just can't.' She bit her lip and continued raggedly, 'I saw a competent, caring man reduced to a paranoid shell who in the end couldn't face another patient. He died of a heart attack brought on by the stress of a legal suit that should never have been processed, and wouldn't have been if it hadn't been for the press's involvement. Do you know what that's like?' she asked as she got to her feet, her hands clenched by her sides. 'To watch someone you love fall apart and, no matter how hard you try, there's nothing you can do to stop it?'

Liam watched as she walked off stiffly towards the car park, her features set. A few moments later her car disappeared down the dirt road, a thin plume of dust coiling up behind her.

He looked down at the food Mavis had heaped on his plate and sighed, wondering if he'd ever had less appetite.

CHAPTER NINE

KEIVA was just finishing some notes on her first patient of the day when Anne McFie put her head around the door.

'Can I talk to you for a second?' she asked.

'Sure.' She closed the folder and pushed it to one side. 'What's up?'

Anne took the seat opposite, her expression troubled. 'Jane told me Mr Holt's body has been transferred to Sydney for an autopsy.'

'Yes. I knew Detective Darcy was going ahead with it.'

'But aren't you worried?' Anne leant forward in her seat, her voice almost a conspiratorial whisper. 'What if...you know...they find something?'

Keiva took in a deep breath and did her best to smile reassuringly at the ward clerk. 'What they'll find is that a sweet old man died of a heart attack.'

'But people are saying...' Anne's hand went to her throat in a nervous gesture and her voice lowered even further. 'He could have been *poisoned*.'

'Come on, Anne,' Keiva said. 'Don't let your imagination get the better of you, like everyone else in town. What possible motive would anyone have for poisoning Mr Holt, or indeed any of the other cases under review?'

'But if it's true, the killer is still out there.' Anne pointed towards the door of Keiva's office, indicating the community outside. 'He or she is out there amongst us and waiting to strike again. It said so in this morning's paper.'

Keiva hadn't as yet seen the *Karracullen Standard* but she could just imagine the hornet's nest Ted Hurst had stirred up. It wouldn't be long before the Sydney press got wind of it and then the red dust of the outback would really hit the fan.

'What else did the article say?'

'There's a copy in the doctors' room,' Anne said. 'Do you want me to go up and get it for you?'

Keiva got to her feet. 'No, don't bother. I'll go and have a quick look myself. Tell John to page me if anything comes in.'

She left A and E and made her way to the doctors' room, her anger steadily building at the way things were being handled. Gossip was just like a rampant disease, she thought. Once it began to spread there was no stopping it and no amount of damage control could fix things. How would she ever get another job in the city with this dark shadow hanging over her? She could hear the interview panel now: 'Ah, yes, Dr Truscott, weren't you working at Karracullen Base Hospital where all those people were being killed off by some mad doctor?' How would she live the stigma down? It didn't matter how innocent she was, she knew people would still indulge themselves with an array of theories about what had gone on.

The paper was on the table, a photo of the hospital on the front with the headlines: MURDER OR MISMANAGEMENT? READ THE FULL STORY WITH AN EXCLUSIVE INTERVIEW ON PAGE THREE.

She turned the page and quickly scanned page three for anything libelous, but it was the usual Ted Hurst-style speculation and scaremongering, fortunately this time without naming any professionals. The interview was with an ex-patient who claimed she had been terrified the whole time she had been in hospital, sure someone was going to come along and bump her off in the middle of the night.

Keiva closed the paper and pushed it away in disgust. Hearing the door open, she looked up to see Hugh enter the room.

'Finished with the paper, Keiva?' he asked with one of his sneering smiles.

'For what it's worth,' she answered, and made to move past him to leave.

'Just a minute.' One of his hands stalled her, his long thin fingers clasping her wrist a little too firmly.

Keiva gave her arm a sharp tug but he must have sensed it coming and counteracted it by pulling her up against him. She collided with his angular body, her stomach turning over with the sudden urge to be ill when she encountered his obvious growing arousal. Her breath was locked in her throat, blocked by the boulder of fear that had lodged itself there.

'Let me go, Hugh,' she said when she could find her voice. 'Let me go or I'll file a report on you that will do more damage to your career than you can possibly imagine.'

He held her flashing gaze for a moment before responding chillingly, 'File any report you like, but I suggest before you do so you should work on clearing your own name in this inquiry.'

She swallowed nervously and hated the fact that he saw it. 'I have nothing to hide. I treated every patient appropriately.'

'Are you absolutely sure about that?' he asked.

'Of course I am,' she insisted, and wished she felt as confident as she sounded. What if she had missed something? No one was perfect and even doctors had bad days...

'What if Detective Darcy's toxicologist finds something untoward?' he asked. 'Who do you think they'll interview first?'

She'd already been interviewed first so that answer was easy, but she didn't bother stating it.

'I think it's best we wait until the toxicologist has something to report, don't you?' she said instead. 'Who knows? Maybe the finger of accusation will be pointed at you.'

His mouth thinned into an aberration of a smile. 'You think me capable of murder?'

The truth was, she didn't know what to think. As much as she loathed Hugh on a personal level, his professional standards were some of the best she'd ever seen. He was meticulous in his diagnoses and follow-ups, and although his bedside manner at times was on the imperious side, she had never yet seen him put a clinical foot wrong.

'I think you're making a big mistake in continuing to harass me,' she said, glancing at his hand on her arm.

He let her go and she resisted the urge to wipe her wrist against her clothes, determined not to show how desperate she was to escape his presence.

'The trouble with young women like you, Keiva,' he drawled. 'You think if a man simply looks at you it's harassment. Tell me, does Detective Darcy get the same brush-off you give me?'

Keiva knew her creeping colour was giving her away but there was little she could do to control it.

'Ah…' He gave her a knowing smile. 'I see how the land lies. A little affair with the detective will take the heat of the inquiry off you, won't it?'

She frowned as she began to comprehend his meaning, her growing anger tightening her voice. 'My private life is no business of yours, nor will it ever be.'

'First it was Campbell, now it's Detective Darcy.' He shook his head in a gesture of disapproval. 'Naughty, naughty Keiva, don't you know good girls don't behave like that?'

Keiva stared at him in complete and utter shock.

'You think…' She cleared her throat to get the words past her choking rage. 'You think I've had some sort of affair with *Campbell*?'

His cold eyes ran over her suggestively. 'Everyone knows he's unhappy with Lana. Ever since the accident…' He paused deliberately. 'She can't give him what he wants, what every man wants—a satisfied woman in his arms.'

Keiva was almost beyond speech. She felt tainted by even being in the same room as Hugh, much less listening to him discuss her closest friend's intimate details.

'Don't look so surprised,' he continued. 'Do you think I don't know what's been going on? Campbell follows you around this hospital like a lovesick puppy. He's gone out of his way to help you settle in because he sees you as a vicarious wife since his own is now out of action.'

'I can't believe I'm even hearing this.' She turned for the door.

'He has a drinking problem, you know.' Hugh's words stalled her outstretched hand as it went for the doorknob.

She let her hand drop by her side as she turned back to face him, her chest feeling as if someone had thumped it. Hard.

'I don't believe you.'

He elevated one greying brow. 'I respect your doubt, Keiva. I realise you need evidence to base your opinions on but, believe me, Campbell Francis is walking…or perhaps I should say, *tottering* a very thin line. If he's not careful, he'll be deregistered if the medical board gets even one whiff of the brandy he keeps in his filing cabinet.'

She wished she could throw his filthy accusations back at him but she'd seen the bottle of brandy herself. In fact, she'd even joined Campbell once or twice in his office at the end of a particularly gruelling day, each of them sipping a small drink before they went home for the evening.

Although she'd never seen Campbell drunk or even a little bit tipsy, she of all people knew of the personal stress he held within him, not to mention the professional demands he faced each day. She struggled with it herself at times. The long hours, the heart-wrenching cases, the vicarious grief she felt when dealing with the recently bereaved and the high stress of handling emergencies all took their toll. Some days she felt like a worn-out towel that had frayed at the edges, all its threads tired, useless and disconnected, unable to perform the duties it had been designed for. Campbell had all that, as well as the guilt he still carried over his wife's injuries, which she and Lana had only discussed the other day.

'Have you considered he could be the one responsible for the deaths?' he asked into the heavy silence.

'No.' Her answer was both immediate and implacable.

His sneer reappeared. 'Such confidence, but you must admit he is the one person in this hospital with unlimited access to drugs. Didn't you read that article in the *Medical Review* about the high correlation found between drug abuse and anaesthetists?'

She had not only seen it and read it, she had also filed it, but she wasn't prepared to admit it to him. She was still frantically thinking of something to say when the pager she was wearing bleeped. Looking down at the screen, she saw she was needed in A and E immediately. She didn't even bother with a parting shot but opened the door and let it click shut behind her, wishing she could close the door so firmly on her troubled thoughts as well.

'We've got another patient for you in cubicle three,' John informed her.

Keiva reached for her stethoscope. 'What's the story?'

'Young woman of twenty-three, acute lower abdo pain. Her husband said she became ill during the night. She looks very pale and sweaty.'

Keiva went to the cubicle where the woman was lying shivering, her husband's face stricken with concern.

'Hello, I'm Dr Truscott.' Keiva gave them both a quick reassuring smile. 'Now, when did the pain first start?'

'Last night,' the young woman answered in a thread-like voice. 'I'd just gone to bed and suddenly got pain low down in my tummy. The pain got worse all night and this morning I fainted when I got out of bed.'

'She's been vomiting,' the husband put in.

'Any other symptoms?' Keiva asked.

The young couple exchanged glances briefly.

'My wife is about six weeks pregnant,' the young man said.

Keiva turned to the young woman. 'You've had a positive pregnancy test done?'

'Yes, two weeks ago. My GP did the test and I'm booked for an ultrasound the week after next.'

Keiva turned to Jane who was standing to one side. 'Jane, we need to put in an IV, get off a full blood count and cross-match and get an ultrasound of the pelvis.'

'Is it the baby?' The woman's face crumpled.

Keiva touched her on the shoulder. 'We won't be sure until we see the ultrasound, but it sounds like you might have an ectopic pregnancy.'

The husband frowned. 'But isn't that life-threatening?'

Keiva did her best to reassure him. 'Not if we act quickly.' She turned back to the patient. 'An ectopic pregnancy is unfortunately not able to progress to term because the fertilised egg becomes trapped in one of the Fallopian tubes.'

The young woman swallowed. 'Will I be able to have another baby in the future?'

'I don't see why not, but for the moment we have to concentrate on managing this situation. If it is an ectopic pregnancy you'll need to have immediate surgery.' She excused herself and went back out to where Jane was speaking on the phone to the radiologist.

Jane put the receiver back down. 'He's on his way.'

'Good, I don't want to wait around on this. She's cold and clammy as it is, probably bleeding internally.'

'I don't think we've had an ectopic for ages,' Jane said. 'It's pretty rare, isn't it?'

'It's thankfully not all that common. Thank goodness there was already a positive pregnancy test—ectopics are unfortunately often misdiagnosed because of the similarity to appendicitis.' She glanced at the clock and frowned. 'How long did you say Corey would be?'

'Here he is now.' Jane turned to greet the middle-aged man who'd just come into A and E. 'Corey, cubicle three. Emma Darlington. Suspected ectopic.'

Corey's eyebrows lifted in unison. 'Haven't seen one of those for a while. Have you lined up Theatre?'

Keiva gave a nod. 'Geoffrey's on his way.'

Once the young woman was transferred to Theatre, Keiva took a moment to gather her thoughts in some sort of rational order by going to her small office and closing the door. She ignored the cold cup of coffee on her desk and pretended not to see the half-eaten chocolate bar from the day before as she sat and stared sightlessly at the food pyramid chart on the wall above her desk.

Hugh had to be wrong about Campbell.

There was no way Campbell would ever act inappropriately at work or even privately, no matter how hard his life had become since Lana's accident. But even she had to admit that as staff anaesthetist he was the one with unlimited access to the IV trolley and drugs, which meant that if Detective Darcy's toxicologist did happen to find a trace of anything in Mr Holt's tissues, the finger of suspicion would be pointed at him first...

Liam was on his way to the hospital when his mobile phone rang. The automatic answering device allowed him to continue driving, the friendly, clear tones of his colleague coming across the four hundred or so kilometres from Sydney as if she were sitting along side him.

'Hey, there, Andrea, got something for me on the body I sent you?'

'I'm afraid not,' Andrea Heyward, the toxicologist, said. 'I've emailed the details of the results in a confidential attachment through to the local police station, but in a nutshell—Mr Holt died of a cardiac arrest.'

Liam frowned. 'Nothing in his blood?'

'Not even a drop of cooking sherry,' Andrea replied.

He let out his breath in a whoosh of frustration, the sound of his fingers drumming on the steering wheel carrying across the phone line.

'You're really stuck on this, aren't you, Liam?' Andrea asked.

'I just have a gut feeling, that's all,' he said.

'Yeah, well, you know what the police manual says about gut feelings—they don't count unless they're backed up by cold hard evidence.'

'Looks like I'll have to get the coroner to authorise the exhumation of the other bodies.'

'We might not find anything in them either,' she said. 'I've been thinking about that case in the States a couple of years back. You know the one where the nurse injected a patient's IV line with too much potassium?'

Liam frowned as he recalled the incident, his next words sounding as if he was reading it from the report he'd seen on it. 'Potassium chloride—an excess amount can trigger a cardiac arrest.'

'And leave absolutely no trace of anything untoward in the blood or tissues once death occurs.' Andrea filled in the rest. 'As soon as there is any cellular breakdown the potassium levels rise, so as far as immutable evidence goes, well, you know the story. There is no evidence.'

'I still want to go with the exhumations,' he said.

'You think that's really necessary?' Andrea asked. 'Is there someone you particularly suspect?'

Liam thought about it for a moment before he answered. 'I'm trying to keep an open mind at this stage.'

Andrea laughed. 'You never like to commit yourself, do you? But surely you must have someone you're keeping a close eye on?'

Liam wondered what Andrea would say if he told her exactly where his eyes were trained, both awake and asleep. Somehow over the past few days shoulder-length chestnut hair and toffee-coloured eyes had filled his mind until he had trouble thinking about anything else, much less the alleged murder case he was supposed to be concentrating on.

'This is a smallish country town,' he said instead. 'I've got my eye on just about everybody.'

'Any nice women out there in the sticks?' she asked.

What is it about happily married women, he thought, that they spent most of their time trying to get everyone they knew hitched as well?

'One or two,' he answered evasively.

He could almost hear the cogs of his friend's brain turning in true feminine inquisitive style.

'What's her name?'

'Whose name?'

'The woman you fancy.'

Liam gave a quick snort. 'Did I say I was interested in anyone? I said there were one or two women out here, that's all.'

'Ye-e-es, but, knowing you as I do, that means you've met someone who has stirred you up a bit.'

Good choice of words, Liam thought privately.

'Anyway,' Andrea went on, 'it's about time you put the Linda episode well and truly behind you and got on with your life.'

'You sound exactly like my mother,' he said.

'Sometimes mothers know best.' There was a tiny pause before she added, 'What does she look like?'

Liam opened his mouth to describe Keiva, but then changed his mind. 'Until I sort this case out, I'm afraid everyone is guilty until proven innocent.'

'So this woman is involved in the inquiry in some way?' Andrea guessed.

'You could say that,' he answered wryly. 'She's the doctor who treated each and every one of the patients who later died.'

'Shoot, Liam.' Andrea's tone turned all serious. 'You're involved with a *suspect*?'

'Not as such.'

'What the hell does that mean?' she asked. 'Liam, come on! Don't compromise yourself. How can you be objective if you're sleeping with the woman?'

'I'm not sleeping with her,' Liam said firmly, but somehow the little word 'yet' seemed to hang in the air, even though he hadn't uttered it.

'Yeah, right,' Andrea said. 'Well, all I can say is, try to keep your head straight. You're a cop, trying to find out if a murder or murders have been committed. That's your main priority, not filling in the time with the best-looking woman in—what's that place called? Karra—'

'Karracullen,' Liam filled in, before adding, 'And how did you know she was the best-looking woman out here?'

Andrea gave an amused chuckle.

'Because you, Detective Darcy, wouldn't settle for anything less.'

CHAPTER TEN

KEIVA had not long come back from checking on Emma Darlington's recovery from surgery the next day when Carol, Campbell's registrar, asked to speak to her in private.

'Sure. Come this way.' Keiva directed her to her small office and waited until the younger woman was seated opposite before she took her own seat behind her desk. 'What can I do for you, Carol?'

The registrar looked at her hands for a moment as if she wasn't sure how to begin.

Keiva felt like drumming her fingers on the desk in impatience. She had little time for Campbell's new registrar, believing, along with Campbell, that she wasn't cut out for the speciality she'd chosen. Along with her slightly surly nature, which she made no effort to disguise from either patients or colleagues, Keiva had seen Carol crack under pressure too many times to be confident she would overcome the tendency once she completed her fellowship training.

'I don't know how to say this…' Carol raised her pale blue eyes to meet Keiva's, an expression of deep concern on her features.

'Just say it, Carol,' Keiva said. 'I have patients waiting.'

The registrar paused for a moment, her cool gaze still fixed unblinkingly on Keiva's.

'Well?' Keiva urged again.

Carol looked back down at her hands for a moment. 'I realise this will be difficult for you since you have such a good working relationship with Dr Francis…' She paused once more and lifted her gaze back to Keiva's wary one. 'But I think you need to know he…he has a problem.'

Keiva forced her expression to remain impassive, though inside she could feel her stomach twisting in alarm.

'What sort of problem?'

Carol seemed to hesitate, her gaze going back to her hands where they were twisted in her lap.

'Come on, Carol.' Keiva got to her feet and came around to perch on the edge of the desk nearer the registrar. 'What's all this about? Is it something to do with your rotation? Campbell and I have been concerned about some of your reactions to—'

'He drinks on the job.'

Keiva felt her blood run cold at the blunt statement, Hugh's earlier words echoing inside her head with sickening clarity.

'Do you have any evidence of him having done so?' she asked as soon as she trusted herself to speak calmly and unemotionally.

Carol's gaze slowly came back to hers. 'He has a bottle of brandy in his desk drawer.'

Keiva let out a breath of impatience as she got to her feet once more. She went back behind her desk and, clutching the back of her chair with both hands, faced the young woman squarely.

'There's a very big difference between having a bottle of liquor in one's drawer and drinking on the job.'

'I thought I should tell you, that's all.' The registrar's expression turned sullen as she too got to her feet. 'I wouldn't want a patient's care to be compromised by one of Karracullen Base's staff acting inappropriately.'

Keiva compressed her lips for a moment.

'Look, I appreciate your concern, Carol, but you and I both know the professional standards of Campbell Francis are extremely high at all times and under all circumstances. He's just too damn good at his job to go jeopardising it in the way you've described.'

'I'm not the only one who's noticed.'

Keiva felt the full force of the registrar's statement as if she'd hit her with it.

'I suppose you're referring to Hugh Methven?' she asked after a tense moment or two.

Carol's pale features washed over with colour at the mention of the senior physician's name and Keiva wondered if he had been giving her a hard time, as he did with just about every other female staff member.

'I had lunch with Dr Methven earlier today and discussed my concerns with him,' Carol informed her proudly and somewhat defiantly.

'I see.'

'He agrees that something needs to be done.'

'I will look into it, but in the meantime I would appreciate it if you kept this between us. I would hate for Campbell's career to go up in smoke over a silly little misunderstanding.' She held open her office door, signalling the end of their meeting. 'I won't keep you from your work. Good day.'

She waited until the registrar was well down the corridor before she closed the door, turning to lean her back on it as if desperate for the support it offered.

'So help me, Campbell,' she muttered under her breath. 'This had better not be true.'

As Keiva was leaving for the day she practically ran into Liam as he came through the front doors of the hospital. He reached out a hand to steady her and the file he had in his hand slipped to the floor at their feet. She watched as he bent down to pick it up and once he'd straightened felt the warm cupping of his hand on her elbow.

'Is there somewhere we can be in private for a few minutes?' he asked in an undertone.

Keiva's heart gave one of its funny little skips at the intensity of his grey-flecked blue eyes. 'Now?'

'Now.'

'Follow me.'

She led the way down the hall towards a small storeroom,

which wasn't being used now that it was after eight in the evening.

Liam closed the door behind them both with a soft clunk, his eyes meeting hers across the small distance between them.

'I have some results for you.'

'Y-you do?'

She knew she looked worried but she just couldn't quite hide the nervous flicker in her eyes as they dipped to the folder in his hands.

'Mr Holt died of a heart attack,' he said.

She didn't bother to disguise her breath of relief. 'Thank God.'

He quirked one of his dark eyebrows at her.

'I mean…' Her tongue snaked out and moistened her lips briefly. 'I meant I'm glad he didn't die by some…some other means…'

'I'm still keen to have the rest of the bodies exhumed.'

Her eyes widened in alarm. 'But…the families. It will be so distressing after all they've been through.'

'The whole issue of murder is distressing, Keiva.'

'But the toxicology report showed it wasn't murder in Mr Holt's case,' she said. 'Doesn't that convince you this is all a fuss about nothing?'

'I'd hardly call the unexpected deaths of the other five people nothing.'

Keiva could feel her temper rising. So he was back in distant detective mode, was he? What had happened to the man who had been kissing her senseless a couple of days ago?

'I didn't mean that. I just think you're going to cause a whole lot of pain for people who have already lost someone dear to them,' she said, somewhat sharply.

His eyes pinned hers. 'Tell me what would happen if someone put too much potassium in a patient's IV line.'

She pressed her lips together as she faced him, a worried look coming back into her eyes. 'Too high an amount of potassium can be just as fatal as having too little.'

'What would happen?' His question was repeated, a little more firmly this time.

'You're the one with the medical science degree,' she said. 'I'm sure you don't need me to tell you.'

'All the same, I'd like to hear it from you.'

She held his determined gaze for as long as she could, wondering where this was leading. Did he really think her capable of deliberately poisoning patients under her care? She knew she should have discussed this possible scenario earlier but…well, he had a distracting manner at times, to say the very least.

'It would cause a cardiac arrest,' she finally answered. 'I was going to speak to you about it…' Her gaze lowered to her twisting hands. 'I remembered hearing about a case…'

'When were you planning on telling me?' he asked.

She raised her eyes back to his at his hardened tone. 'I was going to tell you the day at the gorge…but…but other things were on my mind.'

She saw his jaw tighten momentarily, as if he wasn't sure whether to believe her or not.

'If you don't believe me ask Jane Catchpole or Anne McFie or even Lana Francis. I discussed it with all of them,' she said.

'But you didn't think to mention it to me?'

'I told you I was going to but you…when you kissed me it sort of went out of my head.'

Liam knew the feeling. He was supposed to be doing preliminary investigations, but all he could think about was the young woman in front of him and the way she made him feel. Her melting eyes, her slim curves and that sharp little tongue that he had tempted into softness as it had mated with his.

He closed the gap between them in two strides and pulled her into his arms. 'You are driving me out of my mind, Keiva Truscott, do you know that?'

Keiva could barely breathe for the need to have his mouth on hers, the effort to speak completely beyond her as well. She looked deep into his glittering gaze and released a little sigh of acquiescence as his mouth came closer and closer.

His lips grazed hers, brushing over them like a rough broom sweeping away resistance. She offered none. Her mouth flowered open to the first probe of his determined tongue, and the inner muscles between her legs contracted as if already preparing for his hard male presence. She was melting from the inside out, her body weakening as she leant into his solid frame. All she could think about was how good it felt to be back in his arms, his commanding mouth driving every thought out of her brain until only feeling and sensation coursed through her in great rolling waves.

She felt the slight rasp of his chin on the soft skin of her face as he deepened the kiss even further, her spiralling need for him bursting inside her, leaking into her limbs until she could barely stand.

After a few pulsing minutes he dragged his mouth off hers, his breathing heavy as he looked down at her with eyes ablaze with desire. 'This isn't the right place for what I want to do right now.' His tone was husky and deep. 'Are you free later?'

'How much later?' She was amazed her voice came out at all, much less so calm and controlled.

He smiled down at her, one of his hands coming out to stroke the side of her face, the thick pad of his thumb lingering over the swollen curve of her mouth.

'I'll be at your place in an hour,' he promised.

She smiled up at him and wondered if he could hear her heart kicking in her chest in anticipation.

'One hour it is,' she breathed.

He gave her one last toe-curling look as he opened the door, his eyes relaying a promise she couldn't ignore. Her breath hitched in her throat as the door closed behind him, the air around her closing in on her, each particle seeming to carry a hint of his aftershave and the male heat of his skin until she felt as if she was breathing him into her very body…

She was just about to get into her car a few minutes later when she saw Campbell coming across the staff car park. She opened her mouth to call out to him but when she saw him stumbling towards his vehicle she froze as Hugh's and Carol's earlier words came back to her.

He has a drinking problem.

She closed her car door and moved hesitantly across the car park, wondering how she should handle this.

'Campbell?' she called to him softly, glancing around quickly to see if anyone else was watching, but thankfully all was clear. 'Campbell?' she called softly again, but he either didn't hear or deliberately ignored her as he lurched against his car, his head hanging down as if he was going to be sick. Keiva's own stomach twisted painfully as she moved closer, her heart sinking at the thought of what Lana would say if she saw him like this.

He turned as if he sensed her behind him, although his eyes were glassy and unfocussed. 'What's up, Keiva?' he slurred.

'Oh, God.' She grasped him on the arm to make him look at her. 'Campbell, you can't drive in this state. You're drunk!'

He wobbled on his feet and tried to stare at her, his eyes filming over as he fought to keep her in his line of vision.

'I...I haven't had a d-drink...'

'Give me your keys,' she demanded.

She heard him search for them in one of his pockets but the effort caused him to stumble even more and he began to slide down against the car.

'Oh, for God's sake!' she hissed at him in frustration and anger. 'Get up before someone sees you like this!'

He dragged himself upwards with her help, his head wobbling on his shoulders as if he had no control over it whatsoever. She hunted in his pocket for his keys and pocketed them, the other hand holding him as best she could against the side of his car to stop him falling.

'I can't believe you've done this to yourself,' she railed at him furiously. 'How are you going to explain this to Lana?'

He seemed to momentarily come to his senses at the mention of his wife's name.

'Lana… She's gone…'

'Gone?' Keiva stared at him, her heart thumping against her ribcage alarmingly. 'What do you mean, gone?'

He waved a hand in the air as if pointing the way. 'B-Brishbane…her sister's place…'

She let out her breath in a gush of relief. Lana often went to her sister's home in Brisbane ever since her brother-in-law had passed away, but usually she told her beforehand.

'Just as well. I think she'd kill you if you came home to her drunk,' she said, her tone full of reproach.

Campbell suddenly clutched at her arm, his fingers like bruising clamps. 'Kill who? Kill her?' His eyes rolled in his head like a madman's. 'I would never…d-do that.'

'I know,' she answered, wondering if she even believed it now she'd seen him like this. Campbell was the last person she would have expected this sort of behaviour from. Even Hugh, as loathsome as he was at times, would never allow himself to be on the hospital premises in a state of such heavy inebriation.

'Come on.' She tugged him towards her car. 'I'm taking you home.'

'B-but…' He waved ineffectually at his car parked under the biggest of the paper-bark trees. 'What about my car?'

Keiva gave him a don't-argue-with-me look. 'It can stay there until morning. I don't want you driving under the influence, and, so help me God, when you sober up you're going to get the biggest lecture from me for being so damned irresponsible.'

Campbell tottered along like a newborn foal, his limbs not quite able to keep him upright or even in a reasonably straight line.

Keiva was sweating profusely by the time she pushed and shoved his long angular frame into the small confines of her car. Once he was in and belted, she went around to the driver's door and slid into her seat, her hands tight on the steering-wheel as she turned to look at him slumped against the passenger door.

She sucked in a furious breath and turned the key in the ignition, but nothing happened. She swore, just the once but it was enough to bring Campbell's head up from where he was leaning on the window.

'Something's wrong?' He slipped towards her drunkenly.

She shoved him back against the window and gave the key another turn, praying to every god she'd ever heard of. One of them must have been listening for the car started like a dream. Flashing Campbell a relieved grimace, she turned the car for the hospital exit.

Campbell and Lana lived about fifteen kilometres out of town in an old Victorian mansion that had been meticulously redecorated by Lana's loving touch. The absence of children in their lives had been replaced by an almost obsessive attention to detail in every aspect of the grand old house and extensive gardens. Keiva loved visiting the place—it reminded her of some of the stately homes she'd visited when she'd done a rotation at St Guy's in London. She'd often spent her weekends off roaming the estates of the English countryside. As a result, every time she drove through the wrought-iron gates of Cullenthrop she fully expected a uniformed footman to greet her as her car drew up in front of the house, opening the door for her and sweeping her a bow.

This time no one was there but the almost unconscious Campbell by her side, and as soon as she brought her car to a stop it stalled ignominiously with a choking splutter.

'Come on,' she said as she wrenched open the passenger door. 'You need a vat of black coffee and I need my head read for even bothering to help you.'

'W-where am I?' He looked around dazedly as she helped him from the car.

'You're at home and that's where you and I will stay until I'm sure you're safe to be left alone,' she said, trying not to think about Liam waiting for her at her house.

It wasn't as if she could ring him and tell him she was nursing Campbell through a drunken stupor. Well, she could, but it would mean all hell would break loose as a result, and she wasn't going to let that happen if she could help it. She'd have to think of some excuse—an emergency or something that she had to attend. Maybe, just maybe she could get away with it. A vision of Liam's piercing grey-blue gaze came to mind and she suppressed a little inward shiver.

She'd never get away with it.

She looked down at her mobile phone and for once in her life was glad there was no signal. Just for good measure she switched it off, deciding she couldn't handle any more than one man at a time, and the one currently in her company was proving to be a little more than a handful.

Campbell fell over at the front door and his nose began to bleed copiously, staining the creamy sandstone of the steps just like guilt. She hauled him upright and once she'd found his keys in her pocket and opened the heavy front door, she shoved him through. He stumbled towards the nearest bathroom and she heard him being sick, but decided to leave him to it. She was more angry than sympathetic and for once didn't know how to deal with it.

Disbelief and disappointment were at war inside her, each vying for her attention—disbelief that Campbell would act so self-destructively, and disappointment that Liam would be waiting for her in vain, thinking heaven-knew-what of her for not turning up as arranged.

Campbell came out of the downstairs bathroom looking ashen, his eyes still glazed. 'Keiva?' He blinked a couple of times and wiped at his nose, smearing blood all over his cheek. 'What are you doing here?'

She rolled her eyes and took a step towards him, her index finger outstretched in reproach. 'What the hell are you doing to yourself? You're a doctor, for God's sake! You're responsible for other people's lives. You can't do this sort of thing, especially in a community as small as this. You can't do this sort of thing…' Her voice cracked but she continued anyway. 'You can't do this sort of thing to me…'

Campbell shook his head as if he were trying to clear it of some sort of cloying fog. 'Where's Lana?' he asked, blinking again.

She shut her eyes to avoid looking at him in such a state of disarray. Campbell had been like an idol to her, the one person she could rely on. Steady as a rock—no, a boulder—the one person you could turn to when things were getting out of hand.

'Oh, Campbell…' she began to cry. 'What have you done to yourself?'

He stumbled back towards the bathroom and she turned away in disgust.

It took her almost three hours to get him upstairs and into bed. She left him in his clothes, even though he'd been sick all over himself, because she was too furious with him to do anything about it. She sat and watched him sleep for another hour, deliberating whether it was safe enough to leave him, knowing how easily people could choke on their own vomit when inebriated to this degree.

She decided to stay because she knew that if the boot had been on the other foot he would have done the same. Not only that, she felt she owed Lana this at the very least. Everyone had a bad day at times. Medical personnel were probably more at risk than anyone. And things had been very stressful lately with the inquiry going on.

She sat up straight in her chair and stared at the sleeping figure in the bed, the soft lamplight casting his features into shadow. The thought was in her mind before she could stop it. Could Campbell be responsible for the deaths?

No.

She shook her head as if to rid herself of the stain of the straying thought, but it crept back just like a spreading pool of blood on the floor of her mind.

He had ready access to all drugs and the IV trolley was under his command.

No.

But then she reminded herself she would never have considered him capable of being drunk and disorderly while on the hospital premises. She'd been wrong about that, so what else could she be wrong about? Hugh's words kept coming back to prod her like a small thorn under her skin, each time the pressure a little more difficult to ignore. *Didn't you read that article in the* Medical Review *about the high correlation between drug abuse and anaesthetists?*

She closed her eyes to try and block out the article but it wouldn't go away. It was as clear in her brain as if she'd just finished reading it. The paper had stated the figures on the growing problem, citing the high stress of the job as one of the causal factors, the ready access to drugs another.

Campbell muttered something unintelligible in his sleep and she opened her eyes to look at him, her shoulders slumping dispiritedly at the thought of Lana finding out about tonight. Hadn't the poor woman suffered enough?

Another hour ticked past and since he hadn't made a movement or sound for ages, she went over and checked his pulse, relieved it had slowed to a more normal pace. She wrinkled her nose at the sour smell of his vomit clinging to his clothes, but didn't feel comfortable removing them for him. He would have enough shame to face come morning—that was, if he even remembered a thing about this evening. How many drunken patients had she dealt with during the course of her career who hadn't been able to remember a thing about why they'd ended up in hospital bruised or broken from an accident or brawl? Far too many to be under any illusions about Campbell being any different.

She settled herself back in the chair and closed her eyes once more, wishing she could open them again and find herself inside her own bedroom instead of this one.

She imagined how it might have been tonight with Liam if

she'd turned up as arranged. Her belly did a tiny flip-flop as she pictured him coming towards her, his shirt wrenched out of his trousers, his shoes…one after the other thudding to the floor…his belt being unbuckled…the proud bulge of his maleness pressing against her as he hauled her close…

Keiva woke with a start when a car's headlights swept over the darkened bedroom like twin searchlights. She glanced at her watch and saw it was well past midnight, far too late for someone to be making a social call.

She went to the window, being careful to stay shielded behind the heavy curtains hanging on each side, relieved she'd turned off the bedside lamp the last time she'd checked on Campbell. She frowned when she saw the car moving towards the house along the eucalypt-lined driveway, the long, sleek lines of its darkened shape reminding her of a predatory animal on a silent hunt for unsuspecting prey. The car's headlights were like golden eyes, their piercing beam penetrating the darkness until nothing was left unseen.

Keiva held her breath as the car pulled up behind hers, her heart pounding as a tall figure got out and circled it once, his hand reaching out to feel the temperature of the bonnet as if calculating how long it had been sitting idle. She shrank back against the fold of curtain when his gaze lifted towards hers, as if he knew she was on the top floor, hiding, her guilty secret lying in the bed right near her, just waiting to be exposed.

She was so close to throwing open the window and telling Liam the truth when she heard his car prowling back out of the wrought-iron gates, the long beams of his headlights moving down the driveway, leaving her in total darkness once more…

CHAPTER ELEVEN

'KEIVA?' Campbell struggled upright in his bed and stared at her in confusion. 'What are you doing here?'

Keiva rose from the uncomfortable chair where she'd spent the night and sent him a look full of reproach.

'I suppose you don't remember a thing about last night, do you?' she asked, placing her hands on her hips.

His forehead creased in a frown. Glancing down at himself, his nose wrinkled in distaste at the smell of dried vomit clinging to his clothes. He lifted his troubled gaze back to hers. 'I don't remember much…' His frown increased. 'Have I had some sort of funny turn?'

Keiva let out an impatient breath. 'You call getting plastered before you've even left the premises of the hospital ''having a funny turn''?'

'Plastered…' His eyes widened. 'Drunk? *Drunk?*' He said it twice as if he couldn't believe it himself.

'You made that drunken patient Mr Henty look as sober as a High Court judge,' she informed him coldly.

Campbell's chest seemed to cave in as he lay back on the pillows, his head shaking from side to side in denial. 'But I didn't have anything to drink. I did my rounds, wrote up some notes and dictated a few letters before I left.'

'Come on, Campbell!' Keiva felt like screaming at him. 'You could hardly stand up! Thank God no one saw you, and you have me to thank for stopping you from driving yourself home. God knows what might have happened if you had got behind the wheel of your car.'

The sound of Campbell's agitated swallow filled the silence of the room.

'I didn't have anything alcoholic to drink, Keiva,' he maintained, his voice low but insistent. 'I had coffee at five-thirty—two cups, I think, as I was already feeling tired from taking Lana to the airstrip early in the morning.'

Oh, how she wanted to believe him! Her respect for him was in pieces, and it felt as if each and every one of them was piercing her heart.

'You were drunk, Campbell. Your words were slurred, you were repeatedly sick and you couldn't walk in a straight line.'

'I did not have a drink!' He flung the bedcovers back and stood up somewhat unsteadily as his hands went to his throbbing head.

'Yeah, right.' She sent him a disgusted glance. 'I just hope to God you get yourself sorted out before Lana sees you like this. And as for work, don't even think about seeing patients until you have this under control.'

'I do not have a drinking problem, Keiva,' he said. 'Surely you know me better than that? After what happened to Lana…' One of his hands rubbed over his eyes before he continued, 'Apart from the odd brandy at the end of the day, I hardly touch the stuff. One drink and that's my limit. Please, Keiva, you have to believe me.'

She turned away and reached for her bag on the floor. 'I'm going downstairs to have a cup of coffee. I'll give you ten minutes to have a shower and then I'll drive you back to the hospital to collect your car.'

'Keiva?'

She closed the door behind her and walked down the wide staircase with a heart even heavier than her defeated footsteps.

Hell, what a mess!

Campbell was silent the whole way back to the hospital and Keiva was immensely grateful for it. She wanted time to come to terms with her shattered illusions. Vocalising them any further wasn't going to do any good anyway. Campbell had to get his problems sorted out, and fast. She wasn't going to stick her neck out for him unless she was sure he was serious about dealing with the situation in a responsible manner.

She had only just driven into the car park when Hugh pulled in behind her, drawing his BMW into the space beside hers.

'Well, well, well,' he drawled, as he unfolded himself from the car, taking in Campbell's downcast eyes. 'I never would have thought it of you, old boy. And with Lana away, too. Tut tut tut.'

'Go take a running jump,' Keiva snarled at him. 'Campbell has been…unwell. I offered to drive him home last night.'

Hugh's cold eyes moved from Campbell to Keiva, his cynical smile tilting even further at the dull flush now staining the anaesthetist's cheeks.

'You should see a doctor, Campbell,' Hugh said, flicking his snake-like glance towards Keiva. 'Get her to give you the once-over.'

Keiva knew she was close to completely losing her temper so, snatching up her briefcase from the back seat, she left the two men and stalked towards A and E.

'Detective Darcy wants to see you,' Anne said as Keiva came through the front door. 'I told him to wait in room five, it's more private there.'

'Thanks.' Keiva's tone suggested anything but gratitude and Anne instantly frowned.

'He seemed angry. Did you two have some sort of falling-out?'

She did her best to give the ward clerk a little smile but she knew it wasn't all that convincing. 'I'm guilty of the crime of standing him up last night. I expect he's going to do the whole injured male pride routine. Wish me luck.'

'You stood him up?' Anne's eyes nearly popped out of her head. 'Whatever for? Or should I say, whoever for?'

Keiva gave her shoulders a little shrug. 'You know how it is. I had something better to do.'

'You have definitely been out in the country way too long,'

Anne shook her head at her. 'He's the best-looking guy that walked in that door since…since… Good God, Keiva, he's the best-looking guy who's *ever* walked through it!'

Keiva wholeheartedly agreed but didn't let on. 'Call me if I'm needed.' She shouldered open the door and, moving through, let it swing shut behind her.

Liam eased himself away from the window, where he'd been leaning, as Keiva opened the door of room five.

'Liam, I need to explain about last—' she began.

'Don't bother.' His eyes hit hers—hard. 'I already know about your relationship with Campbell Francis.'

'My what?'

His mouth twisted as he looked down at her. 'You spent the night with him, didn't you?'

'I…' She lowered her gaze slightly, staring at the pulse beating in his tanned neck. 'Yes…I did.'

The silence was so heavy Keiva felt as if she could put her hand out and touch it.

'I did spend the night with him, but not like you think,' she went on after a moment or two. 'He was…wasn't feeling well so I drove him home and stayed with him to make sure he was all right.'

'Didn't his wife mind?'

She forced her eyes to meet his. 'Lana is away at present…visiting a relative. I didn't think Campbell was well enough to be left alone.'

'What was wrong with him?'

Keiva found it nearly impossible to hold his gaze for more than a second or two. 'He was…vomiting.'

'Any other symptoms?'

She compressed her lips, trying to think of a way out of the corner she'd been backed into—mostly by her own stupid misplaced loyalty.

'Keiva?' he probed.

She met his eyes once more, her voice, when it finally came to her lips, not much more than a breath of sound. 'No.'

There was another pulsing silence.

'Why didn't you call me?' he asked. 'I left several messages on your phone.'

'My mobile was out of range.'

'Doesn't Dr Francis have a land line connected at his house?'

'Yes…but I was too busy looking after Campbell and…' She didn't finish the sentence as she realised how weak her lies were on closer inspection. That Liam thought so too was more than obvious by the hardening glitter of his angry eyes.

'I would have appreciated it if you'd just said you weren't interested in the first place,' he bit out.

'I had every intention of keeping our date,' she said. 'It's just that Campbell took me by surprise and I had to deal with his…illness.'

His eyes hardened even further as they pinned hers.

'Has Campbell Francis ever been under the influence of alcohol whilst at work?' he asked.

How was she supposed to answer? Yes, last night, in full view of the hospital as he'd lurched about the car park? But then she reminded herself that he had assured her he had not been in contact with patients, and as far as she knew no other staff member had witnessed his out-of-character behaviour.

'No, I don't believe he would ever do that,' she answered, without looking at him.

'Are you aware he keeps a bottle of brandy in his office?'

Her eyes went to his once more. 'Who told you that?'

His gaze was very intent as he held her nervous one. 'I was interviewing one of the registrars, Carol Duncan. She has been increasingly concerned about Dr Francis's behaviour of late.'

'What do you mean?'

'She told me that Dr Francis has a drinking problem.'

'That's a serious allegation, especially in this sort of profession,' she said.

'Yes, indeed it is, that's why it's imperative that no one—

and I mean no one—covers up for him, if indeed he has been drinking while under the duty of care of others. But apparently Carol Duncan isn't the only one who thinks Campbell Francis has a problem.'

'Oh, really?' She tried to inject her tone with indifference but didn't quite manage to pull it off.

'I also spoke to Hugh Methven, and he informed me of similar concerns,' he said.

His eyes seemed to be challenging her to go on with her version of last night's events, as if he wanted to unpick her fabric of lies thread by thread until nothing was left but the truth.

Keiva felt herself cracking. She now understood why innocent people often found themselves pleading guilty to crimes they had never committed just so they could escape the penetrating probe of investigative eyes that seemed to be able to see past one's flesh and bones to the very soul beneath.

She let out her breath and, unlacing her tightly clasped fingers, faced him squarely.

'All right… I admit I thought Campbell was drunk last night but I can assure you it was completely out of character for him. I've never seen him like that before and I've heard no rumour or suggestion of him having a problem with alcohol before yesterday, when Hugh and Carol both spoke to me. I'm not sure what to make of Carol's opinion but I dismissed Hugh's on the basis of the long-standing professional and personal jealousy he feels towards Campbell.'

'Why did you lie to me?' he asked, his tone sharpened by thinly controlled anger.

'I…' She ran her tongue over her dry lips before continuing, 'I'm sorry… I didn't think… I just wanted to protect Campbell.'

'I take it you've heard the term ''accessory after the fact''?' he asked.

Her colour faded as he continued. 'You don't have to actually commit a crime to find yourself in jail, Keiva. But if a jury finds you've helped someone else do so, you might find yourself looking at four blank walls for a very long time. Do I make myself clear?'

She lifted her chin, pride coming to her rescue. 'What am I supposed to be guilty of? As far as I can see, all I did was help a friend. Or is the fact that I stood you up the thing that really gets up your nose? I saw you out at Cullenthrop last night,' she added bitterly. 'Is that part of your job description? Checking up on me in the middle of the night, as well as during the day?'

His jaw tightened as he looked down at her flashing eyes and rigid stance, all his instincts warning him to get away while he still could. But ever since that very first interview with her he'd felt a magnetic pull so strong he wondered if what he'd felt for Linda had been the genuine article after all. Every time he was within touching distance of Keiva he felt as if his body was on fire, every cell inside him throbbing with the urge to make her his in the most masculine and sexual way possible. Only the fact that they were in a small room in a busy country hospital made him keep control, and then only just.

'I would suggest, Dr Truscott, that in future you are very careful who you try to protect. If one of your colleagues has an obvious problem, the appropriate authorities need to be informed of it.'

'I told you—I don't believe Campbell has a problem,' she insisted, but her tone wasn't as confident as she would have liked.

'You've told me a lot of things, Keiva,' he returned. 'But I'm finding it harder and harder to believe any of them.'

She opened her mouth to defend herself but he'd already brushed past her to make his way to the door, the sound of it snapping shut behind him making her wince.

A and E was particularly busy and Keiva was grateful for the distraction of the long list of needy patients so she didn't have to think about her uneasy relationship with Liam.

Jane met her as she came back into A and E. 'Dan Blacklock has just arrived. You know the guy with the duodenal ulcer you saw a few months back?'

Keiva grimaced as she reached for her stethoscope. 'Don't tell me his wife and kids are with him. The last time was bad enough.'

Jane gave her a grim look. 'They're all here. Can't you hear them?'

She could and it wasn't encouraging. She loved kids but there was no place for six of them in the middle of a busy A and E department.

'Hello, Mr Blacklock,' she greeted the man on the examination table. 'What seems to be the problem?' *Apart from your out-of-control brats and overworked wife,* she thought privately, sweeping her gaze over the Blacklock clan as they began to surge forward.

'He's not going to die, is he?' Louella Blacklock raised her voice over the sound of the baby crying in her arms.

'Mu—um! Darren pushed me,' one of the four boys whined.

'Did not!' The older boy gave his brother a hard shove, which had the domino effect of knocking over one of his sisters standing close by, who immediately let out a howl like a hyena.

Keiva smiled at Louella politely. 'I understand you are all very upset but I can't tell what's going on with all of you in here. Nurse will take you out to the waiting room and I'll be out as soon as I have examined your husband.'

'Come on, Louella.' Jane ushered the family out. 'There's a drinks machine in the foyer.'

Keiva turned back to the patient, who was now groaning. 'Where does it hurt, Mr Blacklock?'

'All over, Doc… I'm gonna vomit.' He began dry-retching.

'Your whole abdomen?' She tucked a bowl under his chin. 'When did it start?'

'This morning…I woke up with it.' He retched again and gaspingly added, 'I'm gonna die, aren't I? What about the kids? I can't die.'

'Calm down, Dan. Now, you've got a duodenal ulcer, haven't you?'

He nodded and clutched at the bowl. 'For years. That high-pressure job of mine. I live on antacids and pills. Been bad the last few weeks. Nothing does any good.'

'Let me have a feel of your tummy,' Keiva said as Jane took over the bowl-holding.

John came in from one of the other cubicles, where he'd been tending to a minor laceration. 'What's up?'

'Dan has an acute abdomen, John. Generally tender, rigid and guarded, rebound, no bowel sounds.'

'I'll organise an X-ray,' he said.

The X-ray came back a short time later and Keiva put it up on the screen. 'Look, free gas under the diaphragm. Most likely a perforated ulcer.' She turned back to Dan. 'Looks like your ulcer might have perforated, Dan. You'll need surgery. I'll put in a drip and get Theatre organised. You'll be in good hands with Geoffrey Ellerton.' She gave his leg a gentle reassuring pat. 'I'll come up and see you once you're out of Recovery. And don't worry about the family. I'll get the ward clerk to rustle up some sandwiches from the kitchen.'

Keiva worked her way through the list of waiting patients with a doggedness brought on by trying not to think about Liam. Her feelings about Tim seemed so pathetic now. She could barely recall Tim's features and yet she had only to think of Liam and he filled her entire headspace until she could think of nothing but grey-blue eyes and a mouth that delivered on its promise of passion every single time…

'Keiva?' Jane gave her a nudge as she handed her the chart she'd asked for. 'Are you with us or on some other planet?'

'Sorry?' She gave herself a mental shake and took the clip-board from Jane with an apologetic grimace. 'I was just think-ing about something else…'

Jane ushered her into an empty cubicle and twitched the curtain around them. 'What is it with everyone today? You've been spacey all day and now Campbell's gone all weird on me as well.'

Keiva's hands on the clipboard froze. 'What do you mean, Campbell has been acting weird?'

Jane gave a little shrug. 'I don't know…he just doesn't seem himself. All glassy-eyed and funny. His hands were shaking when he put in Mrs Baker's IV line while you were on your break. I've never seen him do that before. Is he unwell?'

Keiva looked away before Jane could see how much her words had shaken her. Surely Campbell hadn't started drinking at work? It wasn't even three in the afternoon.

'Maybe he's just missing Lana,' she offered, pretending to be inspecting the notes in front of her. 'You know how much he worries about her.'

'You could be right,' Jane agreed. 'But what's your excuse? You've been off with the fairies most of the day, staring into space with that far-away look in your eyes.'

'I have not!' Keiva protested.

Jane folded her arms and smiled. 'You're in love with him, aren't you?'

Keiva kept her head in the notes. 'I suppose you're referring to Detective Darcy?'

'Who else?'

Who else indeed? Who else could have rocked her world in such a short time, turning her head and her heart with the very first touch of his hand in hers?

Yes, she was in love with him. Probably had been halfway there when he'd asked her his first question. His first kiss had sent her over the edge and after that swim at the gorge…

'There.' Jane clicked her fingers in front of Keiva's face. 'You're doing it again.'

'Don't be ridiculous.' She handed Jane the notes and pushed aside the curtain. 'I'm going upstairs to check on Joshua Freeman. Call me if there's any action down here.'

Joshua Freeman was sitting up in bed, reading a motoring magazine, when she came into the four-bed ward.

'Hi, Dr Truscott.' He put the magazine to one side.

'How are you feeling?' she asked, pulling the curtain around the bed. 'Have the tics settled down?'

Joshua was a fifteen-year-old who suffered from Tourette's syndrome. Although he hadn't been previously considered a severe case, his symptoms had increased during puberty, making his tics almost unbearable on occasion. Keiva knew he'd been the brunt of ridicule many times until she'd gone to the local high school and done a presentation on the condition. She'd described to the other students that the condition caused sufferers to exhibit certain tics, such as shrugging, blinking, grunting and sudden body movements as in limb jerking. Although medication could help dampen down the worst of the condition, it offered no permanent cure. Joshua had coped well until recently when his symptoms had increased to the point where his normal activities had become almost impossible. He had been admitted under Hugh and given an IV dose of midazolam, and his oral dose of haloperidol had been increased under close observation to help him ride out this difficult phase.

Looking at him now, Keiva wondered how anyone could ever make fun of such an engaging young man. His wide smile and clear blue eyes were irresistible, and although she saw his shoulder shift in a slight tic once or twice it appeared as though the storm was well and truly over.

'I'm much better.' He grinned at her. 'But Dr Methven wants me to stay in another few days.'

Keiva suppressed her frown. Hospital wasn't the place for healthy young teenagers and although he'd had a very rough time recently, it was more than obvious he was well clear of it now.

'And you're OK about that?' she asked, glancing at his medication chart.

'I'm a bit bored,' he admitted. 'But the nurses are nice and the food…well, you know about the food.'

She smiled. 'Are they giving you enough?'

He gave her a sheepish look. 'I could kill for a pizza but at least the tics have settled down a bit.'

She perched on the end of his bed, her glance flicking to the bandage around his hand where his IV line had been the previous day. 'It must be very hard for you, Josh.'

He gave another shrug, this one nothing to do with an involuntary tic. 'It could be worse. I could be paralysed or something.'

His courage moved her deeply and she had trouble keeping the emotion from her voice. 'You're a champion, Josh. Most people would buckle under with what you've had to face.'

'I'm OK.' His cheeks washed with colour and his fingers began plucking at the sheet covering his long legs. 'I knew this kid way back in primary school…he had diabetes. He had to have injections all the time.' He gave a little shudder. 'I hate injections.'

'I don't like them much myself,' she admitted. 'I can give them to other people without flinching, but you should see me at the blood bank, it's truly pathetic. And as for tablets, well, unless they're smaller than a pea I get them stuck halfway down.'

Josh's smile was empathetic. 'I'm fine now. I've been on three tablets a day for a couple of days. Three at once was a bit much, I had to have one of the nurses thump me on the back when I almost choked on them.'

Keiva's gaze went back to the chart in her hands, her forehead creasing in concentration. 'You've been on three a day for a couple of days?' she asked, looking up from the notes.

'Yeah, Dr Methven changed the dose the day before yesterday. I hated being so groggy all the time so I guess he eased back on the dose.' He crossed his fingers and added with a smile, 'So far so good.'

Keiva resisted the urge to inspect the notes once more, hoping she had simply misread them. Giving him an answering smile, she got to her feet. 'I'm glad you're feeling better. I'll try and come and see you again before you leave.'

'Thanks, Dr Truscott.'

She pushed the curtain back and, taking his chart with her, went out to the nurses' station down the corridor.

Sally Cordwell and Rena Taylor, the medical ward nurses on duty, looked up from where they were sitting at the desk as she approached.

'Hi, Keiva, we didn't see you come in. Can we help you with anything?' Rena asked.

Keiva wasn't entirely sure which was the best way to handle the situation she found herself in, but it had to be cleared up one way or the other. The discrepancy with what was on Joshua's drug chart and what he had told her had to be sorted out, even if heads were about to roll.

'I was just talking to young Joshua Freeman about his medication,' she said. 'He told me he's been on one tablet three times a day for the past two days, but according to Dr Methven's notes he reduced his dose only this morning.'

Sally frowned and looked across Rena's shoulder to where Keiva had placed the chart for them to inspect.

'We've not long come on duty,' Sally informed her. 'We haven't done the medications for this afternoon but I could call Juliet, who was here for the last two days, and ask her what she gave Joshua.'

Keiva stood to one side as the phone call was made, her brain whirling with possible explanations—none of them particularly reassuring.

Sally replaced the receiver and swivelled her chair back to face Keiva. 'Juliet insists she put three tablets out, four times a day as directed for the last two days.'

'Did she see Joshua take them last time?'

'I asked her that but she said Dr Methven was doing his rounds with one of the registrars at the time and she just placed them in the plastic cup on Josh's table.'

Keiva pursed her lips in deep thought.

'You think he's lying?' Rena asked.

'Who, Josh?' Keiva asked.

'Who else?' Sally and Rena spoke in unison, their expressions full of consternation.

Keiva picked up the chart once more and gave them both a quick smile. 'Leave it with me. I'll have a chat with Hugh to clear it up. Perhaps Josh is still a little confused after the big increase in medication. Two days on IV midazolam is enough to confuse a mallee bull, let alone a fifteen-year-old boy.'

The nurses didn't answer but Keiva couldn't help noticing the concerned glances they exchanged when they didn't think she was looking.

She went straight to Hugh's office and gave the closed door a sharp rap with her knuckles.

'Come in,' he called from within.

She opened the door and closed it firmly behind her, the sound of it clicking shut bringing his head up from the journal he was looking at.

'Ah…Keiva, what a lovely surprise.'

She approached his desk and laid Joshua's chart on top of the medical journal he'd been reading.

'I was wondering if you could clear up a little matter for me.' She met his eyes with gritty determination. 'There seems to be a mistake in Joshua Freeman's medication doses.'

Hugh leaned back in his chair, his gaze sliding over her leisurely before looking down at the chart. 'He's back on his normal dose, one tablet three times a day. It's there in black and white.'

'Joshua told me you changed his dose two days ago, but this chart documents the change in dose was only made this morning.'

'Did he?' His thin lips stretched into one of his sneering smiles. 'And I suppose you believed him?'

'Why shouldn't I believe him?' she asked.

'He's a kid, Keiva, What would he know anyway?'

Keiva stared at him in outrage. 'He has Tourette's, for God's sake! He's a perfectly normal and trustworthy kid and you damn well know it.'

Hugh rose to his feet and frowned down at her. 'What are you implying? That I've made some sort of mistake?'

Keiva held her ground. 'According to this chart and what Joshua told me, twelve tablets are unaccounted for.'

'I suggest you check under his pillow or wherever it is that teenage boys hide things before you come barging in here accusing me of whatever you are accusing me of!' he stormed.

'Why are you keeping him in hospital? He has no need to be here now his tics have eased.'

'I am his physician, not you,' he barked. 'Now, get out of here before I call Barry Conning and tell him that not only does he have an incompetent A and E doctor on the payroll but a drunken anaesthetist as well.'

Keiva felt herself stiffen with anger. 'You have no proof. You can say what you like about Campbell, but unless you have clear evidence of anything untoward, you haven't got a leg to stand on.'

'What makes you think I don't have proof?' He reached for the drawer of his desk, his cold eyes holding hers as he opened it and took out a digital camera small enough to fit in the palm of his hand.

Keiva stood staring down at the tiny silver camera for endless seconds, her mind whirling with thoughts of what damning images it might contain. She couldn't help thinking that Hugh held not only the camera in his hand but the future of Campbell as well.

And not just Campbell's future, she reminded herself uncomfortably.

Hers as well.

CHAPTER TWELVE

'DO YOU want to see the pretty pictures, Keiva?' Hugh asked with a curl of his thin lip. 'There's rather a nice one of you with your arms around Campbell as he's slumped up against his car.' He pressed some buttons on the camera as if scrolling through to a particular shot. 'Ah…there it is. I wonder what Lana will say when she sees it.'

Keiva wished she had the courage to snatch the camera from him. She longed to stomp her foot on it and smash whatever images he had documented there.

'Why are you doing this?' she asked through tight lips.

He smiled coolly. 'I can't have you saying nasty things about me without some sort of insurance policy, now, can I?'

Her eyes flicked to the drug chart on his desk but just as she moved towards it he placed his hand over it. 'You can leave that with me,' he added. 'I will speak to the charge sister about it.'

Keiva knew she had no choice but to back down. It all rested on a teenager's word against a senior physician's, and it didn't take her long to figure out who Barry or any other medical personnel would believe.

'Come now, Keiva,' Hugh cajoled. 'Why the sour look? Can't you and I be friends just for once, hmm?'

She turned on her heel and stalked out without replying, knowing that if she allowed a single word out past the stiff line of her lips her career would be well and truly over.

When her shift was finally finished Keiva made her way out to the staff car park, her gaze automatically going to where Campbell's car was usually parked. She wasn't sure if she should be feeling relieved or worried when it wasn't there.

She unlocked her car and got behind the wheel with a weary sigh. She turned the key in the ignition, offering up a quick prayer to whoever was on duty, but there was no response from either her car or any magnanimous spirit lurking about.

She allowed herself one swear word and gave the key another turn.

She tried another curse, louder this time, but still the car refused to start.

She got out and slammed the driver's door with all the force of the pent-up anger of the day. 'Have I told you lately how much I hate you for doing this to me?' she asked the tired-looking vehicle. 'I just want to go home—is that so much to ask? Why can't you just do what you're supposed to do and start, for heaven's sake?'

She heard a soft chuckle from behind her and swung around in embarrassment, her colour firing up yet another notch when she saw Liam standing there watching her, an amused smile lighting his eyes.

'Don't ask.' She sent him a warning look. 'Just don't ask.'

He closed the distance between them, his smile still in place. 'Want me to have a go?'

She stepped aside, waving for him to go right ahead. She watched as he got in behind the wheel, his long legs taking up all the available space so he had to adjust the seat to accommodate them. He turned the key and pumped the throttle at the same time, but nothing happened.

'Trouble, Detective Darcy?' she asked with a quirk of one of her eyebrows.

'Could be.' He reached forward to unclip the bonnet. 'This baby doesn't sound so healthy. Did you have it serviced, as I suggested?'

She avoided his eyes as he got out of the car to lift up the bonnet. 'I've been meaning to but I just didn't get around to it.'

She heard him fiddling with the engine but resisted the urge to stand a little closer. She didn't trust herself not to encircle his lean waist with her arms and melt herself against his solid warmth. His clean male smell seemed to fill the evening air, a hint of musk, a hint of citrus and something else she couldn't quite place.

The bonnet snapping shut brought her gaze back to his. 'You can't fix it?'

He shook his head as he wiped his hands on his handkerchief. 'I think your best bet would be a tow truck or, even better, a new car.'

'Yeah, right.' She rolled her eyes at him. 'When do I have time to go and choose a new car?'

He tucked his handkerchief into his back pocket. 'Looks like you're going to have to find the time. You can't be without a car out here. When's your next day off?'

'Did you happen to see any car dealers on your way into Karracullen?' she asked him.

His mouth stretched back into a smile. 'Good point. What about your next weekend off? I could drive you down to Sydney. I have to go back soon anyway.'

She couldn't stop her frown in time. 'You're closing the inquiry?'

He gave her an ironic look. 'Isn't that what you think I should do?'

'What about the exhumations? Aren't you going ahead with them?'

'I've discussed it with my people in Sydney, and on the basis of the findings on Mr Holt they've decided that unless there is a particular direction from the families involved we'll leave things as they are.'

Keiva wasn't sure why she was feeling so disappointed. She'd been so adamant that nothing was amiss, that the deaths could be easily explained, but now...

'Come on.' His deep voice broke across her thoughts. 'I'll give you a lift home.'

'I can call a taxi.'

'You can if you like, but I was going to call on you tonight anyway, so you may as well come with me.'

'More questions, Detective Darcy?' she asked as she fell into step beside him as they walked to where his car was parked.

He gave her an unreadable look as he opened the passenger door for her. 'Get in, Dr Truscott.'

'Say please.' Her eyes locked with his.

His mouth tilted at her. 'You want me to beg?'

Hot colour suffused her face. 'No…of course not. I was just…' She didn't finish the sentence for fear of betraying herself. What was wrong with her? Where was her self-control and professional poise?

She got into his car and made a business of putting on her seat belt, keeping her eyes down. She heard him get in his side and sneaked a look at him, but then wished she hadn't as she encountered his direct gaze.

'Hard day?' he asked.

She moistened her mouth, watching in mesmerised fascination as his eyes followed the movement of her tongue across her lips.

'Y-yes…' She cleared her throat and said it a little less breathily, 'Yes. It was one of those days when all I could think about was getting into my bed at the end of it.'

He started the engine with a growling rumble that she felt through the soles of her feet, his slow burning smile melting her from the inside out as he put the car in gear.

'I was thinking the very same thing myself,' he said, and began backing out of the space.

She looked down at her hands and wondered why they weren't already shaking with anticipation at what he'd just said. It certainly felt as if the rest of her was. Her thighs in particular were buzzing with sensation as if she could already feel him prising them apart to accept him. Heat coursed through her, great tongues of flame igniting her in every secret place until she could barely sit still in her seat.

He turned the car for the exit, the silence beating like a heavy pulse between them.

'I was a bit rough on you earlier.' His voice, when he finally spoke, contained a touch of gruffness.

'That's all right.' She flicked him a quick glance. 'I've had much worse.'

His eyes connected with hers briefly before he turned back to the road ahead. 'I was genuinely worried about you last night. When you didn't show up as arranged, a hundred scenarios ran through my mind.'

'I understand. I'm sorry I didn't call and explain.' She bit her lip. She could just imagine the sort of grisly scenarios he'd seen first hand, she'd seen them herself. It had been wrong of her not to offer him some excuse. She'd been a coward, as simple as that.

'When I finally tracked you down at Campbell Francis's place, I didn't give a thought to any other explanation other than you'd got a better offer,' he said after another pause.

'I've told you, Lana and Campbell are my closest friends.' She swivelled in her seat to look at him. 'How many times do I have to say it to convince you?'

'I guess it's another one of my occupational hazards,' he said. 'I find it hard to take people at face value, especially if they've lied to me before.'

'I'm sorry about lying to you, but I was so concerned for Campbell…'

'Has it occurred to you he might not have been drunk?' he asked after a slight pause.

Keiva stared at him again. 'Not drunk? What do you mean, not drunk?'

He gave a loose shrug as he turned into her street. 'Did you do a blood alcohol test on him?'

'No… I didn't even think of such a thing, and even if I had he might not have been all that agreeable. I just escorted him home and made sure he and the rest of the community were safe by keeping him from driving.'

'Did he smell of alcohol?'

She frowned as she considered his question. Campbell's behaviour had been such a shock to her she had barely managed to think at all, let alone assess the situation from a professional standpoint. When she'd seen him lurching about the car park, slurring his speech, she had immediately assumed he had been drinking. But now that she stopped to think about it, she couldn't recall smelling any liquor at the time. Later, when he'd been sick, the stench of vomit had more or less confirmed her assumption that he had been acting under the influence of alcohol. But had she missed something?

She met Liam's focussed gaze across the width of his car once he'd parked the car in front of her house. 'I don't recall smelling alcohol on him. I just assumed he was drunk because of his behaviour.'

'His very-out-of-character behaviour, I think you said—right?'

She nodded. 'He was slurring his words and falling over himself. He didn't seem to be in a rational state of mind so I decided to take responsibility for him.' She pinched the bridge of her nose and closed her eyes. 'Hell, I wish I could just erase last night and start over.'

Liam stretched out his hand and lifted the curtain of her hair off the back of her neck, his cool fingers resting on her overheated skin. Keiva opened her eyes and looked at him, her heart coming to a standstill when his thumb roved over the soft swell of her bottom lip.

'Do you know what I think we should do right now?' he asked.

She shook her head, unable to locate her voice.

He stroked the upper curve of her mouth with the tip of his long index finger, slowly, lazily.

'I think we should go out to the gorge and have a swim,' he said, staring at her mouth.

'A swim?' She blinked at him.

His mouth tilted. 'You're hot, I'm hot, the evening's hot and the water out there is cool. How about it?'

She could think of nothing better than having a refreshing dip at the gorge. It had been in the high thirties all day and her shirt and trousers were sticking to her in all the wrong places. To feel the silk of cool water over her after such a stressful day would be bliss, and with Liam Darcy with her it would be nothing short of heaven.

'I'll go and get my bathers.' She fumbled for the doorhandle behind her, but his hand came down and stilled on hers.

'You don't need them, just a towel.' His grey-blue gaze held hers. 'I'll wait for you here.'

'Won't you come in?' She managed to open the door at last.

He shook his head. 'If I follow you into the house we both know there'll be no swim to cool off.'

She sucked in a ragged breath and left him waiting in the car, her hands diving for her house keys in her bag as she made her way to the front door.

Don't rush, she reprimanded herself. Don't look so frantic and excited. Play it cool.

Yeah, right.

She unlocked the door and stepped inside. How was she supposed to be feeling relaxed and cool when she hadn't shaved her legs in a month?

She kicked off her work shoes and almost popped the buttons on her shirt as she struggled out of it on her way to the bathroom. Her trousers hit the floor as her hand located the razor and she set to work, trying not to think about how in the city she used to have a beautician to wax away her worries. Karracullen had a beautician, or so she'd heard, but she'd never had the time to seek her out, or any reason to make an appointment as she hadn't once thought about dating until Liam had come into town.

'Damn!' She stared down at the bright streak of blood trickling down her shin where she'd nicked the flesh.

She hopped to where the tissues were and pressed one to the

site, her other hand scrambling through the disordered contents of her bathroom cupboard for a sticky plaster.

'Oh, for pity's sake,' she berated herself out loud as she peered into the cupboard. 'Surely you've got a plaster in here somewhere. You're a doctor, for heaven's sake!'

'Can I help?'

Keiva spun around to see Liam standing in the doorway, a grin splitting his face.

She was standing in her underwear...her *yellowed been-in-the-wrong-coloured-wash-for-too-long underwear*. Not only that, she was dripping blood onto the tiles under her feet. And if that wasn't enough, she'd only managed to shave one leg.

'Can you give me a minute?' She did her best to sound cool and composed, as if she regularly had men standing in the doorway of her bathroom, watching her depilatory routine.

'Take your time. I'm in no hurry.'

She swallowed as he leant against the doorjamb. There went her chance to close the door.

'OK...' She reached for another tissue and dabbed at her shin, relieved to see it had finally stopped bleeding. 'I suppose you think this is highly amusing?' She addressed the tiles at her feet to avoid looking at him.

'Are you talking to me or the floor?' he asked.

She tossed the used tissue in the small bin and raised her eyes to his. 'I know you probably think it's weird, but lots of perfectly normal people talk to themselves.'

His eyes danced with amusement as he folded his arms across his broad chest. 'You don't say?'

She rolled her eyes and reached for the razor once more. Turning her back, she tried to pretend he wasn't there as she stretched out her leg. 'Excuse me, but I have some unfinished business to see to.'

His hands—his cool, dry hands—came to rest on her shoulders, the gentle but firm pressure of his fingers turning her round to face him.

She looked into his eyes and felt something shift deep inside her at the gleam of desire she could see reflected there.

'Excuse me…' He took the razor out of her numb fingers and placed it on the vanity behind her. 'But *I* have some unfinished business to see to.'

Keiva drew in a sharp little breath as his head came down as if in slow motion, her lips swelling in anticipation of the pressure of his. She felt herself lean towards him, her body in the magnetic field of his, pulling her closer and closer, millimetre by millimetre.

His lips brushed hers, softly at first as if tasting her, reminding himself of the shape and feel of her mouth. She felt him stir against her as he drew her even closer, his body leaping to life in response to her softness.

'I want you so badly,' he groaned against her mouth. 'I was going crazy in the car, waiting for you.'

'Y-you were?' She gazed up at him.

He stroked his tongue over her bottom lip before answering, 'Crazy.' He moved to her top lip and added, 'I might have even got to the talking-to-myself stage if I'd stayed out there a moment longer.'

'It must have been the heat…' Her eyes dipped to his hovering mouth. 'You know how hot it's been. It's enough to send anyone a little crazy.' She brushed her mouth against his, once, twice, three times.

His eyes darkened with desire at her butterfly touch and, pressing her backwards against the vanity, he captured her mouth determinedly.

Keiva felt the bold thrust of his tongue through the partition of her lips as it searched for hers, inviting it to dance intimately with his. Scorching need raced through her at the insistent pressure of his mouth, the sweep and glide of his tongue inciting her desire for him to an unmanageable level. Her hands were at his shirt, her fingers fumbling over buttons until she finally found the heated skin of his muscled chest, her fingertips catching on the sprinkling of male hair. She let her hand follow its narrowing trail down to the waistband of his trousers, her fingers aching to touch him without the barrier of clothes.

Liam's hands skimmed up her body, shaping her from hips to breasts, his mouth locked to hers. She felt his hand reach behind her to deftly release the worn clasp of her bra. The tired garment slipped soundlessly to the floor and she shivered in reaction as her freed breasts spilled into his waiting hands. He lifted his mouth off hers to look at the creamy flesh he'd exposed, his thumbs rolling over each tightly budded nipple until she could barely draw in a breath.

He lowered his head until his mouth was on her right nipple, his tongue rolling over the peak, the hot moistness of his mouth like a brand on her.

She felt the hardened ridge of his body straining against the fabric of his trousers, the sheer potency of him urging her on to release him to her exploratory touch. She undid his belt and then his waistband, her fingers tracing his rigid outline through the overstretched fabric of his underwear.

Liam pulled her away from the vanity and, scooping her effortlessly into his arms, carried her through to her bedroom, nudging the door open with his foot in a purposeful manner that sent her blood racing through her veins at breakneck pace.

They landed in a tangle of limbs on the bed, his pressing weight on her a delicious burden, making her thighs go weak with need.

She felt him kick himself out of his trousers, vaguely registering the thud of his shoes when they hit the floor as his mouth came back to hers.

She kissed him with a flare of passion she hadn't thought she possessed, every nerve in her body on high alert under the onslaught of his fiery touch.

He peeled away her threadbare panties as if they were gossamer lace, letting them join his clothes on her floor. She felt his hands on her intimately, his long finger tracing the seam of her body fringed with soft curls, and she thought she would die from the pleasure of it. She wanted more. She wanted him inside where she ached. She wanted him to fill her with the thickness of his need, taking her to the high summit of satisfaction she craved with every leaping pulse of her body.

He eased himself off her briefly, which brought a look of stricken panic to her face. Surely he wasn't going to stop now?

He gave her a sexy smile as he leant over the edge of the bed to retrieve something from his trousers on the floor.

'We can't go past the point of no return without this.' He held up the small foil packet he'd taken from one of his pockets.

'No…I guess not…' She drew in a prickly little breath as she saw him apply the condom to his turgid length, the sheer size of him making her insides turn over. During the course of her career she'd seen the naked male form so many times she'd more or less made her mind up that it was a case of seen one, seen them all.

She'd been wrong.

Her heart began to race, her skin tingling all over at the promise in his eyes as he came back over her, his weight supported on his arms on either side of her.

He looked down at her, words unnecessary as she lifted her head for his kiss. She heard his harsh groan just before his mouth joined hers, his body coming down hard and heavy on hers in all the right places.

She felt him slip between her thighs, one of his hands moving down to guide himself between her tender folds with a gentleness that surprised her, considering his heightened level of arousal. She pushed thoughts of Tim's rushed rough handling aside and concentrated on the slow but sure glide of Liam's body as it joined intimately with hers.

Her breath escaped on a sigh of pure pleasure as he sheathed himself completely, filling her as if made for her and her alone.

He began a slow rocking rhythm that sent quivers right through her singing flesh. She instinctively tightened around him as if determined to hold him there for as long as she could. She could feel pressure building within, a nerve-stretching pressure that begged for release. He increased his pace in response to her soft moans, her hips rising to meet the downward movement of his as she sought the paradise that beckoned.

She began to feel tight all over as she got closer and closer, each deep thrust of his body within hers sending arrows of delight to every nerve ending. As if sensing her approaching orgasm, he tilted her pelvis to increase the pressure of his body, his hand moving to the tight pearl where her pleasure had gathered in preparation for the final plunge into ecstasy. The sensual stroke of his fingers on her sent her over in great rocking waves that made her feel as if she was being tossed about on a sea of pleasure so wide and deep and limitless she had trouble holding on to consciousness.

She felt his heavy breathing still momentarily, the tightening of his large frame over hers as he gave one final groan, signalling his release. She felt the pulse of it within her where her muscles had been stretched to accommodate him, and even though he wore a condom she was sure she could feel his life force pooling within her intimate warmth.

He eased his weight off her and, disposing of the condom, turned to her and gave her a somewhat rueful look. 'That was a little fast. I'm sorry. Next time I'll take my time.'

'Am I complaining?' She stretched languorously, her limbs feeling boneless as she smiled up at him.

He pressed a soft kiss to the side of her neck, moving his mouth around slowly until he planted light as air kisses all over her face, before finally coming back to her mouth.

Keiva felt the slow moving stroke of his tongue within the recesses of her mouth, its action sending spirals of building pleasure to her curling toes and back. She could feel the hardening of his body against her as he moved back over her and it thrilled her that she could stir him into arousal so soon after satiation.

She angled her head to meet his eyes. 'You don't need a rest?'

His eyes burned as they held hers, and she couldn't help

feeling a tiny feathery shiver move over the surface of her skin as she lay in his arms, waiting for his next move with breathless anticipation.

'Later,' he murmured, and caught her mouth once more.

The hectic pace of their earlier coupling slowed to a low burn, like the embers of a banked fire gradually being stirred to fervent life.

Keiva had been sure that her previous pleasure had been as good as it could ever get. She'd certainly never felt such mind-blowing sensations rocketing through her body before and fully expected their second bout of love-making to imitate the first. But again she'd been wrong. The first time had been fast and furious, as they'd each clamoured for release. The second time Liam set a leisurely, exploratory pace, as if he wanted to intimately acquaint himself with every angle and plane and secret crevice of her body. His mouth had been magic on hers each time he'd kissed her. But when he moved down to the feminine folds where her need for him pulsed, she was totally unprepared for the sensations he released in her with the slight rasp of his tongue on her most intimate place.

She arched her back and clawed at the hair of his head as he continued his sensual movements, until the moans she was trying to contain became high cries of unbearable feeling. Her body seemed to be an entity of its own. She had no control over it when Liam touched her in such a way and it left her limbs weak, as if the bones had been disconnected from each other, leaving her limp with total relaxation in his arms.

'Good?' He smiled at her as he moved back up her body.

She nodded, not sure she could even find the words to describe what she'd just experienced. Instead, she ran her hands over his body, her fingers trailing over him in intimate detail, her eyes locking with his when she finally came to his erection.

She took him in her hand and squeezed, her stomach kicking with excitement at the way he responded with a guttural, entirely male groan.

'Was that OK?' she asked, smiling with newfound confidence.

'What do you think?'

She tiptoed her fingertips down the length of him and then back up again to the moistened tip. 'I think that you are very dangerous when armed.'

'Dangerous, eh?' He put his hand over hers to still her action. 'At this point in time, baby, I am unarmed, which is even more dangerous.' He gave her a quick grimace of regret. 'That condom was the last one I had, and unless you've got a supply handy this show is going to be over.'

Keiva knew his sense of responsibility was highly commendable. She'd seen a few too many unplanned pregnancies during her O and G term, not to mention the devastation some women felt after having an abortion. But ever since she'd broken up with Tim she hadn't bothered to keep condoms handy, having never expected to be attracted to anyone enough to sleep with them, or at least not out here in Karracullen.

'I'm sorry...' She looked up at him, her hand still around him intimately, his hand loosely covering hers. 'I didn't expect to...' She lowered her eyes, her colour heightening.

'Hey.' He hitched up her chin so she had to meet his gaze. 'I didn't expect to either. Although I must admit as soon as I met you I knew I was in trouble.'

'You did?'

'You bet I did.' He eased himself up on one elbow to look down at her, a soft smile playing about his mouth. 'You're exactly the sort of trouble my mother has been warning me about for years.'

'Oh, really?' She traced the length of his breastbone with an idle fingertip, her eyes still locked on his. 'What did she say?'

He captured her hand before it went any lower and held it to his chest. 'That one day I would meet someone who would challenge me in every way possible.'

Keiva drew in a little breath that seemed to come all the way up from her hollowed stomach.

'Did you feel that way about your last girlfriend?' she asked.

He picked up a strand of her hair and coiled it around one of his fingers. 'Linda was very attractive but it wasn't until she broke it off that I realised how I'd short-changed myself. She wasn't interested in me as a person. She wanted a perfect life, the money, the house and the regular hours. I couldn't offer it so she went to someone else who could.'

'You must have been hurt.'

He gave a shrug and released her hair. 'I was, but for all the wrong reasons. Pride played too big a part in how I felt about her leaving.'

'Did you love her?'

He ran a fingertip down the length of her nose and smiled ruefully. 'A bit I suppose. What about you? Did you love your fiancé?'

'I did until he betrayed me. I guess that can't have been the real thing, right? If I'd truly loved him, I would have forgiven him, no matter what.'

'My mother would say that genuine love cannot be nurtured unless trust is in good supply.' He rolled off the bed and reached for his jeans.

'You're leaving?' Keiva wished her tone hadn't sounded so disappointed but she just couldn't help it.

He turned to face her as he zipped up his jeans. 'Didn't I promise you a swim?'

'Yes…but…'

'So get out of that bed and come with me to the gorge.'

'Now?'

'Now.' He held out a hand to her and, once she'd put hers into it, hauled her upright, his hands cupping her bottom to hold her close. 'Any further questions, Dr Truscott?'

She smiled as he bent his head to hers. 'No further questions.'

CHAPTER THIRTEEN

THE water of the gorge was alight with the silver streak of the moon across its surface, the fringe of bush along the banks cast in shadow.

'It's so quiet…' Keiva found herself whispering as she joined Liam by the water's edge.

'A nice quiet, though,' he said, and heeled himself out of his boots.

'Sometimes there's so much noise and activity going on you forget what true silence sounds like,' she said, lifting her head to look at the myriad stars blinking down at them.

Liam's hands came to rest on her shoulders from behind, the solid warmth of his body brushing hers with an intimacy that sent her pulse soaring.

'Are you going to get out of those clothes by yourself or am I going to have to undress you?' he asked as his mouth nuzzled against her neck.

'I'm not sure getting undressed is such a good idea.' She turned in his arms and looped hers around his neck. 'Neither of us has any protection and you know how tempting it will be…'

'You could be right.' His smile was wry. 'But as it's so hot, let's swim anyway. You keep to one side and I'll keep to the other, OK?'

'I think I trust you a little more than that.' She laughed.

He gave her a sexy grin and unzipped his jeans. 'You shouldn't trust me at all, sweetheart. I'm just hoping this cold water will do the trick.'

She watched him wade into the water, the moonlight on his back making him seem like a statue that had come to life in the witching hour.

'Is it working?' she called out as she stepped out of her clothes.

'Not so far.'

She walked to the water towards him, her hands covering breasts and her hair about her shoulders. She saw him approach, the silver water parted by his strong thighs as he drew close.

'I thought you were going to stay on that side?' she said.

His hands came around her waist and gently pulled her towards him, his hair-roughened body rasping along the silk of hers.

She closed her eyes to his kiss, her toes curling into the silty mud at her feet as his tongue encircled hers in an erotic dance that mimicked what their bodies had enjoyed the hour before.

His hands cradled the gentle weight of her breasts, his thumbs brushing over her engorged nipples as his mouth worked its magic on hers, driving every thought out of her mind. She was all body and all feeling, her need of him rising like a tide within her, threatening to break through the banks of self-restraint she'd so proudly clung to in the past.

Liam dragged his mouth off hers and took a ragged breath, holding her away from him. 'You might have been right about the clothes.' He gave her a rueful grimace. 'I don't seem to be able to control myself around you.'

She smiled and stepped back into his embrace, rubbing herself up against him with a sensual roll of her hips.

'Now, that is definitely not playing fair,' he groaned against her mouth.

Keiva closed her eyes as he took her bottom lip into his mouth, drawing on it gently before running his tongue over it in a sweeping motion that sent a river of delight to her feminine core.

She had already decided, condom or not, she was going to let him make love to her when she heard the distant roar of a car travelling at high speed on the gravel road beyond the fringe of bush that sheltered them from view.

Liam heard it too and lifted his head. 'Looks like we might be in for some company.'

She opened her mouth to reply when there was the sound of brakes grabbing savagely at the gravel, the rough slide of wheels sounding like a scream of terror, the final metallic crash when it came ripping through the still night air with heart-stopping finality.

'Quick!' Liam rushed from the water and tossed her jeans towards her. 'Get dressed. That sounded serious.'

Keiva needed no other urging. She was already struggling into her T-shirt and caught her jeans as they sailed past, stuffing her wet legs into them before searching for her shoes.

By the time Keiva had joined him on the roadside Liam had already pulled his car up close behind an old model utility which looked as if it had taught several generations of Karracullen teenagers to drive. It was hugging a tree in a grue-some metallic embrace, the engine steaming in protest, the driver's door flung open as if tired of its occupant's presence.

'I've got a first-aid kit in the back,' Liam said. 'Pull it out and get over to them while I set the car up so no one runs into us. I'll radio for help.'

Keiva did as he'd directed and then sprinted back to the car wreck, only to pull up short as a familiar sandy-haired and freckled-faced teenager appeared from the passenger's side, her eyes wide with shock as she stumbled towards her.

'Oh, my God! Cassie, are you all right?'

Cassie began to sob. 'I told Jason to slow down... There was a kangaroo... He wasn't wearing a seat belt...'

Keiva held Cassie away from her and inspected her quickly but surely, relieved to see she had no visible signs of injury that needed immediate attention.

'Listen, Cassie. I need to see to Jason right now. Can you wait in Detective Darcy's car for me?'

'Is Jason all right?' Cassie asked, clutching at Keiva's arms. 'He's not...dead, is he?'

'No,' Liam answered calmly, from the other side of the

wrecked car. 'But I need Keiva around here so I can radio for help.'

'I'll go and take a look at him,' Keiva reassured Cassie as she settled her in the back of Liam's car. 'I'll be right back.'

Jason was lying on his back groaning with pain, a pool of bright blood rapidly collecting under his right leg from a gash across his groin.

'He's going to be OK, Cassie,' Keiva called out reassuringly, her quick glance going to Liam. In a quieter tone she added, 'We've got to stop this bleeding. Something has sliced open an artery in the groin.'

'I'm going to vomit,' Jason groaned. 'I feel faint. Everywhere hurts like hell… What happened? I can't…I…'

'He's white as a sheet, losing blood fast and in shock.' Keiva answered Liam's questioning look. 'Is that ambulance on its way?'

'Not far off,' he said. 'What can I do to help?'

'He's just passed out. You'll have to manage his airway while I stop the bleeding.'

'Onto it.'

As she opened the first-aid kit Keiva couldn't help admiring Liam's quiet competence as he swept Jason's tongue forward, holding his chin to maintain his airway as if he'd done it many times before.

She found the scissors in the kit and began to cut through Jason's jeans, where she found arterial bleeding from a nasty gash. She took out a wad of pads and applied them with hard pressure over the wound and couldn't help a sigh of relief as the bleeding began to slow immediately.

The sound of sirens coming nearer and nearer announced the arrival of help.

'You did well,' Liam said as the ambulance officers loaded Cassie and Jason into the back of the emergency vehicle.

'So did you.' She gave him a grateful look.

One of the local police officers came over once he'd finished taking the necessary photos for the accident investigation team. He took down a quick statement from both of them and once that was done turned to face Liam. 'I hear you're leaving us tomorrow, mate. Had enough of the bush?'

'Time to move on,' Liam said. 'Head office wants me on another case in the city.'

Keiva felt her anger rising as she heard the exchange. Why hadn't he told her he was leaving the next day? Why let her think they still had time to conduct some sort of relationship when he clearly had no such plan?

'To tell you the truth, I never did think we had any crackpot killers out here,' Colin said. 'Got to do the investigation, though, to make sure, I suppose.'

'Yes, all in all I think it was worthwhile,' Liam agreed.

Worthwhile? Keiva inwardly seethed.

Colin's radio receiver began beeping. 'I'd better push on. I've got another call, some drama or other at the pub. Hell, I hate nights.'

Keiva grimaced in empathy. 'Me too.'

Colin shook Liam's hand and raised his hat at Keiva before making his way to the police vehicle. He turned back to them just as he opened the driver's door. 'I nearly forgot. The young lassie said something about a kangaroo. Did either of you see it?'

'I'll go and take a look,' Liam offered. 'It could be still lying about injured.'

Keiva waited until Colin had driven off before she walked across to where Liam was searching a few metres away, his torch beam illuminating the bush lined roadside.

'Find anything?'

Just then the beam of his torch settled on the heaving form of a large grey kangaroo, its eyes wide with pain and fear, its severe injuries making it impossible for it to escape.

'Turn your back,' Liam instructed grimly as he reached for his gun where he'd tucked it in the waistband of his jeans.

Keiva did as he told her, wincing as the sound of a bullet

being discharged rent the stillness of the night. She heard the sound of the kangaroo's body being dragged further into the bush and then Liam's footsteps on the gravel as he came towards her.

He saw the tears spring up in her eyes as she turned to face him. 'I had to do it, there was no other choice.'

'I know...'

He led her back to his car and helped her in. 'I'll just give the gorge a quick sweep with the torch to find anything we left behind.'

She sat in the car and waited for him to return, her thoughts going over the events of the evening, each scene replaying itself in her mind, like some sort of surreal dream.

Shame scalded her from the inside out. She had acted so impulsively and irresponsibly, her principles pushed aside in the quest for the pleasure Liam had offered. Pleasure, yes, but not commitment. She knew he was still smarting from his break-up with Linda, he'd told her as much. This evening had, no doubt, been more about using her as a salve to his male pride than anything else. A quick country fling—that was what he would tell his friends and colleagues. A bit of fun to pass the time. And she had fallen for it like the gullible fool she was. Hadn't her time with Tim taught her anything about the motives of men?

When Liam came back he tossed what appeared to be his underwear on the back seat and joined her in the car.

'You OK?' he asked as he pulled down his seat belt to clip it in place.

'I'm fine,' she answered stiffly. 'But I need to go to the hospital. Could you drop me off on your way home?'

'Sure, but do you really need to be there now? The surgical team will manage Jason from now on.'

'I know. I just feel I'd like to be there to speak with Cassie's and Jason's parents,' she said.

'Fine. I'll drop you off but I'll wait for you.'

'No…please, don't bother. I could be a while. I'd rather be alone.'

Liam frowned as he completed the distance to town. He was being summarily dismissed and he didn't like it.

'Can I see you tomorrow or am I to assume you are going to be too busy?' he asked, not quite able to remove the sharpness from his tone.

'I would have thought it would be you that was too busy,' she said. 'I mean, with having to drive back to the city and all.'

Liam concentrated on the road in front of them, his hands tight on the wheel. He was in no position to reveal his movements to her without clearance from Head Office first. No one was supposed to know he was going to hang around and lie low for a few days while he did some behind-the-scenes follow-up on a hunch he'd had brewing for days.

No one.

'I take it you're upset I didn't tell you I was going tomorrow?' he said.

She didn't even look his way when she spoke.

'Why would I be upset? I knew you were a blow-in right from the start.'

'What about tonight?'

She sent him an expressionless glance. 'What about it?'

His frown deepened as he turned back to the road. 'I thought it might have meant something to you.'

'Oh, it did,' she said, her tone hard. 'It's not every day one gets laid by a visiting detective. I can't wait to tell everyone all about it.'

He let out his breath, his fingers on the steering-wheel rigid with tension.

'Glad to be of service,' he bit out.

Keiva thought it wisest not to respond to his little dig and waited in stony silence until he pulled up in front of the hospital.

She unclipped her seat belt and met his angry glare as she reached for the door. 'Thanks for this evening. It was—'

'Don't insult me by saying it was nice,' he ground out before she could finish her sentence.

'I wasn't going to say it was nice.'

'What were you going to say?' His eyes were cold and the line of his mouth bitter.

She got out of the car and for the sake of her pride smiled down at him through the still open passenger window. 'I had fun tonight. That's what I was going to say. Lots and lots of fun.'

He turned away in disgust and revved the engine to signal he was finished with her, but Keiva wanted the last word and was determined to have it.

'Drive safely, now, won't you, Detective?'

He drove off with such speed the spinning tyres sent a shower of gravel over her feet, but she didn't look down to inspect the damage.

There was no point because she couldn't see for tears.

After spending a few minutes in the staff bathroom in an effort to restore some sort of order to her appearance, Keiva made her way to talk to Cassie and her parents who were waiting with the Hendersons for news of their son.

'Have you heard anything yet?' Cassie came rushing forward as she approached.

'No, but it shouldn't be too long.' She turned to greet the adults and did her best to reassure them that Jason's injuries were under control. 'It was a nasty wound but Geoffrey Ellerton is a fine clinician. He'll have him back to normal in no time.'

'We're so grateful for what you and the detective did out there,' Mrs Henderson said, wiping at tears. 'He could have died.'

Keiva squeezed the older woman's shoulder. 'But he didn't.'

She turned back to Cassie. 'Has someone in A and E checked you out?'

Cassie nodded. 'Apart from a few bruises, I'm OK.'

'That's because you were wearing a seat belt,' she said. 'Maybe you'll have to give that young man of yours a firm talking-to.'

'I will,' Cassie promised.

Keiva left the little group a few minutes later to make her way to her office, not sure she wanted to face the emptiness of her cottage just yet with all its memories of earlier that evening.

She opened the door and came face to face with Carol, who was just coming out from behind Keiva's desk.

'Did you want something, Carol?' she asked.

The young woman met her direct look without flinching.

'No. I thought I heard someone moving about in here so I came in to check.'

'Didn't you think to call the switchboard?'

'No, I didn't see the point.'

'Well, next time I'd prefer it if you did.' She opened the door wider to indicate it was time for the registrar to leave. 'By the way, isn't it a bit late for you to be here? I thought you were on afternoon shift?'

'I had to see Hugh Methven about something.'

Keiva pursed her lips for a moment and shut the door once more. 'Listen, Carol, a word of advice. You might think that socialising with men like Hugh Methven will in some way advance your career, but let me assure you it won't. He's a notorious womaniser and you'll only get hurt in the end.'

Carol gave her a defiant look. 'I know what I'm doing.'

'I hope to heaven you do, but don't say I didn't warn you.'

The registrar brushed past her with a sullen scowl, her usually pale face suffused with colour.

Poor kid, Keiva thought as she closed the door behind her. She remembered a time when she too had been starry-eyed and infatuated with the odd specialist she'd trained under. But fortunately for her no one had seemed to notice or, if they had, hadn't made it apparent. However, in Hugh's case, Keiva knew he would have no such scruples. He would have Carol for breakfast and not think twice about it.

She sat down at her desk and reached for the half-eaten chocolate bar she'd left in her drawer earlier. Thick runny caramel was exactly what she needed right now to remind herself of how she'd been sweet-talked into bed.

She peeled back the wrapping and lifted it to her mouth, but at the last moment stopped. She gave it one last look, turned in her chair and tossed it in the bin, dusting off her hands afterwards.

'You're just not worth the calories, Detective Darcy.'

As she was coming out of her office a little while later she saw Campbell coming down the corridor towards her.

'Keiva, you're here late. Can I have a quick word?'

'Sure.' She led the way back into her office and turned to face him as he closed the door. 'How did Jason's surgery go?'

'He'll be fine. I heard you had something to do with his rescue. Lucky kid. Twenty minutes' bleeding from that artery would have bled him out.'

'I know.' She suppressed an inward shiver. 'I nearly died myself when I saw Cassie get out of that car. It makes it so much harder when you know them personally.'

'Tell me about it.' He gave an empathetic sigh as he reached for the nearest chair and sat down.

Keiva perched on the edge of her desk and gave him a direct look. 'How are you, Campbell?'

'Fine.'

'I mean, how are you really?'

He ran a hand through his hair and sighed. 'I hate that you still think I was drunk that night.'

'Do you have any other explanation?'

'No, I don't.' He shifted his gaze from hers. 'I guess I should be thankful you didn't file an incident report on me.'

'I was tempted, I can tell you.' She hopped off the desk and moved around to her chair, waiting until she was seated to add, 'I found Carol Duncan in my office a few minutes ago.'

'Oh? What, waiting for you?'

'No.' She let out a small breath and continued, 'She said she heard someone moving about in here and came in to check.'

'And was there anyone in here?'

She shook her head. 'I had a quick look around after she'd gone but nothing seemed out of place.'

Campbell frowned. 'I must say I've been finding her a bit of a worry lately. She hasn't got her mind on her work and seems overly emotional at times.'

'I think she fancies herself in love with Hugh,' Keiva said.

'Yes. I had noticed a certain something going on between them. Speaking of which…' he gave her a teasing wink '…how is Liam Darcy?'

Keiva felt her face heating and lowered her gaze to her hands in front of her on the desk.

'He's leaving tomorrow morning. The inquiry is closed. End of story.'

'I thought he and you were…?' he left the sentence hanging.

'Well, we're not,' she said bluntly.

'Shame. I thought he was a decent sort of chap.' He gave a short rueful laugh. 'Asks a lot of questions, though.'

'Yes…'

'Keiva?'

'I'm fine about it, Campbell, really.' She met his concerned gaze.

'You haven't got all that long out here now,' he said. 'Maybe you could look him up when you get back to Sydney.'

'I don't think so.'

She got to her feet and went to look out the window, the almost deserted car park suddenly reminding her of how late it was. She turned back to look at him. 'Can you give me a lift home? My car has decided it's taking some long service leave.'

Campbell gave her a wry smile as he got to his feet. 'You sure you trust me enough to drive?'

'The way I feel right now, Campbell, I wouldn't mind if an axe murderer offered me a lift. I just want to go home.'

'Well, since Karracullen is apparently all out of axe murderers and serial killers, I guess I will have to do,' he said with a grin.

'Very funny.' She gave him a reproachful glance as she led the way out. 'But I only hope to God you're right.'

CHAPTER FOURTEEN

As KEIVA'S taxi drove past the Bullock and Dray the next morning she prided herself on not even glancing to see if Liam's car had gone. She'd spent a restless night agonising over how she'd handled her relationship with him, wondering if there had been anything she could have done to avoid the hurt she was currently feeling, but had decided in the end it was yet another lesson well learnt.

Her pain over her break-up with Tim seemed so distant and insignificant now—what she had felt for him a vague memory that was increasingly difficult to bring to mind. And yet she only had to think of Liam and the way his questioning eyes had held hers, and her skin would prickle all over with remembered sensation.

She paid the fare and made her way to A and E, where Jane was waiting to speak to her, the expression on her face indicating it was urgent.

'Keiva, I've been waiting for you to arrive. Come into the storeroom where it's private. I have something to tell you.'

Keiva followed her into the small room and closed the door behind her. 'What's going on?'

'I had to drop some patient notes up to Hugh Methven's office a few minutes ago.' She took a steadying breath and continued, 'He was drunk, Keiva. *Drunk!* At eight in the morning. I couldn't get a word of sense out of him. Can you believe it?'

Keiva frowned. 'Is he still there?'

Jane nodded. 'I just left the notes and closed the door. What's Barry going to say? Think of it! Hugh Methven! The high-and-mighty-never-puts-a-clinical-foot-wrong Hugh.'

'Have you mentioned this to anyone else?'

'No, I thought I'd speak to you first. What should we do?'

Keiva compressed her lips for a moment as she collected her thoughts then, finally coming to a decision, she headed for the door as she instructed Jane over her shoulder, 'I want you to come up to his office with a pathology kit. Don't make it too obvious. Just bring one up as soon as you can. I'll go right now and check him out.'

'A path kit?' Jane's forehead wrinkled in confusion. 'For heaven's sake, he's drunk, Keiva, not anaemic.'

'I want to run a few tests on him before I make my diagnosis. Just do as I say and don't speak to anyone about this until I tell you.'

'You think I don't know drunk when I see it?' Jane looked affronted.

'Let's just do it my way, OK? We're talking about a person's professional reputation here. We need to establish the facts before we go reporting something that could very likely have some other explanation.'

'What other explanation could there be?' Jane asked.

'That's what I'm about to find out,' she said, and left the room.

She didn't bother knocking at Hugh's office door. She checked the corridor for anyone passing by and once it was clear turned the doorhandle.

He was slumped at his desk, an empty bottle of brandy near his left hand, the strong alcohol fumes hitting her as soon as she stepped inside.

'Hugh?'

She approached the desk, stepping over a puddle of what appeared to be even more liquor soaking into the carpet.

She turned his wrist over and felt for a pulse, somewhat shocked to find it was erratic.

Jane came in at that moment with a pathology tray, her expression full of reproach.

'Hand me his stethoscope—over there,' Keiva instructed. 'I want to listen to his chest.'

As Jane helped sit Hugh more upright in his chair, it was clear to Keiva that he was deeply unconscious.

'Support his head,' she instructed Jane as she loosened his tie and unbuttoned the top of his shirt.

She was shocked to see that Hugh's jugular venous pressure was clearly elevated, indicating cardiac failure. She placed the stethoscope over his chest to reveal a gallop rhythm and rapid atrial fibrillation and then, as she listened at the lung bases, discovered there were fine crepitations.

'Hugh is in rapid AF, Jane, and cardiac failure. I've never known him to have any cardiac disease, and I've never seen alcohol do that before. Give me the tourniquet and red-, blue- and white-topped blood tubes. I'm taking a full range of bloods, as well as a drug and alcohol screen.'

'Toxicology?' Jane's eyes widened. 'You think he's doing drugs as well?'

Keiva released the tourniquet and took off her gloves before answering.

'I don't know what he's done but I know it's serious. I want him admitted immediately to CCU with full cardiac monitoring. He'll need an IV line and we'll need to get his cardiac failure and rapid rhythm under control.' She tossed her gloves in the bin and added, 'I've put "Urgent" on this blood form, Jane. Get an orderly to get them to Path, stat, and get some A and E staff up here to watch him while I get CCU organised.'

'Right.' Jane rushed out with the pathology tray and Keiva reached for the phone on Hugh's desk and pressed in Campbell's number. He answered on the third ring.

'Keiva? What are you doing ringing from Hugh Methven's extension?'

'Campbell, listen to me.' She kept her eyes on Hugh the whole time she was speaking. 'I'm admitting Hugh to CCU.'

'CCU ? What's wrong with him? What's happened?'

'I don't know. I'm running blood tests on him right now, but he's in rapid AF and cardiac failure.'

'Cardiac failure? Hugh Methven ?' He whistled through his

teeth. 'I told him to give up smoking. Look, I'll inform staff and so on, and the medical super—'

'No, Campbell, not yet. I want to keep this as quiet as possible for now.'

'Quiet? What on earth for?'

'I don't know…' She gnawed at her bottom lip a couple of times before continuing, 'There's something about all this that doesn't seem right.'

'What do you mean?'

Keiva stared at the empty bottle on Hugh's desk for a moment, trying to assemble her thoughts into some sort of working order.

'Keiva?'

'What label of brandy does Hugh usually drink?' she asked after another short pause.

'Brandy?' Campbell gave a snort. 'Hugh doesn't drink brandy. He's a Scotch man. You know what a snob he is. He'd rather die than drink anything else.'

'That's what I thought,' she said, her frown increasing.

'Look, I'd better come up and take a look at him,' Campbell said.

'Don't bother,' she said. 'The trolley's just arrived. Meet me in CCU. I don't want to run any risks until I know exactly what's going on.'

Campbell joined her a few minutes later as Hugh was being hooked up to an ECG monitor and pulse oximeter.

'Anything on the bloods?' he asked.

'Not yet.' She watched the screen readout for a moment. 'His heart is all over the place. I though he was in rapid AF but there are extra systoles in there and… Look at that, Campbell, he's just had a run of VF.'

'This is worrying, Keiva. How long has he been unconscious?'

She checked her watch. 'I don't know exactly. Jane found him just after eight this morning. She thought he was drunk.'

'And you don't?'

She turned to look at him, 'I've made this mistake before, Campbell. I'm not going to make it again.'

'Here are some blood results,' Jane came towards them with printouts.

Keiva glanced through them, her frown deepening. She handed them to Campbell, her eyes communicating her concern.

He flipped through the forms and let out a single swear word when he came to the toxicology report.

'Halperidol! What the hell's he on that for? And look at the level. That's a hell of a way above the toxic range.'

Keiva took him to one side out of the hearing of the CCU staff.

'Listen, Campbell, I found a discrepancy on one of Hugh's patients' drug charts the other day. I spoke with him about it but he seemed defensive and I let it go.'

'What are you saying?' Campbell frowned. 'That he's feeding some sort of addiction?'

She glanced sideways again to make sure no one was picking up their voices and continued in a hushed tone. 'No. Think about it, Campbell. Hugh is a pain in the butt and a complete womanising jerk most of the time, but for all that he is a competent and ethical clinician. He just doesn't make mistakes, and he's no drug addict. And, anyway, have you ever seen an addiction to halperidol? It's a brute of a drug with a load of unpleasant side effects. It just doesn't make sense. Why would he do this to himself?'

'But if *he* didn't administer the drugs, who did, and how?'

Keiva was still thinking about her answer when the ECG monitor screamed a high-pitched alarm.

'He's had a cardiac arrest! He's in VT!' she shouted as she rushed across. 'Staff, Call code blue, CCU. Get the resus trolley!' She turned to Campbell. 'Bag and mask him while I start cardiac massage.'

As the crash trolley was rushed in, Keiva pumped on Hugh's

chest five times to Campbell's artificial respiration using a bag and mask.

'I'm going to shock him, Campbell. Nurse, give one ampoule of lidocaine IV, stat. OK, charge the defibrillator to 100.'

Keiva ceased her cardiac massage and applied the paddles to Hugh's chest, sweat breaking out on her brow.

'*Clear!*' She pushed the button on one of the defibrillator paddles, and Hugh responded with a back-arching convulsion. The cardiac monitor momentarily flat-lined in response to the DC current, but then the VT rhythm reappeared.

'Come on, Hugh, don't do this to us!' she begged.

'Where the hell is Carol?' Campbell barked at one of the nurses. 'She should be here, helping.'

'We're losing him.' Keiva glanced at the monitor. 'Come on, Hugh, don't give up.' She took a calming breath to cool her panic. 'Thirty seconds more cardiac massage to get that lidocaine around and I'll cardiovert again.'

'Keiva, his oximetry is 70 per cent. I can't oxygenate him with a bag. If you can't cardiovert him this time, I'll intubate him,' said Campbell.

'OK. Turn the defib up to 150, Nurse, and charge. Ready, Campbell? OK. *Clear!*'

Again Hugh writhed with the shock of DC current and the cardiac monitor briefly flat-lined.

'Look, Campbell. We're in sinus rhythm! Blood pressure, Nurse?'

'One-ten systolic, Dr Truscott.'

'We did it, Keiva.' Campbell flashed a quick smile of relief her way. He turned back to Hugh. 'Look, he's still very drowsy. I'm going to sedate and intubate him, and we'll get him round to ICU on a ventilator till the haloperidol wears off.'

'Yes…' She bit down on her lip to control her post-stress emotions. 'That was close—too close…'

Campbell busied himself with the nursing staff while Keiva stepped out into the corridor to take a few deep breaths. She found Jane leaning against the wall, her usually tanned face tombstone white.

'Are you all right?' she asked.

Jane looked through the open door at Hugh lying a few feet away and shuddered. 'I can't stop thinking about what would have happened if I hadn't found him when I did.'

'Don't think about it, Jane. You did find him in time and we sorted it out.'

'I know but…but what if you had taken my word for it and left him there to sleep it off?' She sent another tortured glance in Hugh's direction.

'Come on.' Keiva took her arm and led her away. 'Let's get back to A and E. Lord knows how many patients are banked up, waiting for us.'

The rest of the day passed without further drama, which relieved Keiva no end. She could handle the odd broken bone and lacerated finger, but after the tension of the morning felt as if anything more serious would have sent her over the edge.

She checked on Hugh several times, but although he was off the ventilator he still hadn't regained consciousness. She was glad in a way, for she didn't envy the person who would be assigned the task of telling him what had happened.

At the end of her shift she made her way back up to ICU and sat by his bedside, not sure why she felt the need to do so. She didn't like the man but in a way she felt sorry for him, recognising that behind his overbearing exterior he was really, when all was said and done, a very lonely person.

She was just thinking about leaving when the curtain of his cubicle was twitched aside and Carol appeared. Something about the young woman's manner unsettled her. She seemed on edge, her movements jerky and her eyes darting all over the place in agitation.

'Is something wrong, Carol?' she asked.

The registrar turned to look at her, the ice of her eyes making her even more uneasy.

'I want to be alone with him,' Carol said. 'Please, leave.'

Keiva stayed seated, refusing to be ordered about by a junior. She hated pulling rank but Carol was one person she had never liked and she didn't see why she should move aside, given she'd been more or less responsible for saving Hugh's life.

'I think I'll stay, if you don't mind,' she said.

'I do mind,' the young woman snarled. 'Get out. He's mine, not yours.'

Keiva shrank back from the venom in the registrar's tone, her eyes going to what she held in her hand like a weapon.

'Get away from him.' Carol stepped towards her, brandishing a syringe. 'He doesn't want you, he wants me.'

Keiva stood up and eased herself out of the tight space with caution, her eyes never leaving the wildness of the registrar's.

'Carol, this is crazy. I don't have any interest whatsoever in Hugh.'

Carol's face crumpled. 'You lying bitch! He won't look at me while you're around. I thought I was safe while you were with that detective but now he's gone you're going to take Hugh off me. I just know you will. *Get back*!' she screeched as Keiva stepped forward. 'Get back or I'll give you what I've given each of your patients.'

'*What?*' Keiva stared at her in horror.

Carol laughed and waved the syringe above her head. 'Aren't I clever? You never guessed, did you? You think you're such a great doctor but you know nothing. Nothing, do you hear me?'

'Oh, God,' Keiva gasped. 'You killed Mr Holt and the others?'

'You bet I did.' Carol pushed the syringe in her face. 'And you are next.'

Keiva fought for time, hoping someone would hear what was going on behind the screen of Hugh's curtain, but ICU was a noisy place at the best of times and she was fast losing hope.

'So…' She made her tone as casual as she could. 'How did you do it? I mean, it takes some brains to hoodwink the whole medical profession, not to mention a hotshot detective from the city.'

Carol's eyes shone with pride. 'I know. But I thought it through very carefully. Potassium chloride is untraceable in body tissues. It's the perfect crime.'

'What about Hugh?' Keiva asked. 'How did you medicate him?'

The registrar's expression went from pride to anger. 'He wouldn't have dinner with me. He said he wasn't interested any more. I crushed some haloperidol into his coffee.'

'So it was you who changed the drug doses.'

'Hugh was furious with you for accusing him.' Carol smirked. 'But when he saw the chart he assumed he'd made a mistake. Those were his initials there but I put them there, not him. I practised for hours to get it right.'

'And the brandy?'

Carol laughed again. 'Wasn't that a stroke of genius? I made it look like he'd been drinking.'

'Where did you get the brandy?'

'From Dr Francis's office.'

Keiva eyed the syringe and forced down her panic. 'What about Dr Francis? You medicated him, too, didn't you?'

Carol's expression turned even uglier with hatred. 'He didn't get the full dose. I wanted to pay him back for all the times he's told me off.' She gave a maniacal laugh. 'Hugh thought he was drunk and took photos.'

'I suppose you had something to do with that?'

Carol's eyes hardened to chips of ice. 'Of course. Why wouldn't I? Campbell Francis doesn't think I'm good enough. I thought I'd show him just how good I am.'

'What do you plan to do now?' Keiva asked. 'You seriously can't expect to get away without being found out?'

'The detective has called off the inquiry,' Carol said. 'I had to wait until he left, you see. I didn't want him to catch me.'

'You've thought it all out,' Keiva said. 'It must have taken a lot of meticulous planning.'

'Yes…but you've been the spanner in the works.'

'Oh? In what way?'

Carol's eyes blazed with fury. 'You didn't eat the chocolate.'

Keiva frowned in confusion. 'The chocolate?'

'I spiked your chocolate bar with the rest of the haloperidol,' Carol informed her proudly.

'That was clever,' Keiva said, even as her stomach rolled. 'Everyone knows how much I love chocolate.'

'I know. I told you I was clever but you've never thought so, have you? You've always thought I wasn't up to the task, just like Dr Francis, didn't you?'

Keiva felt as if her legs were going to go from beneath her. She was rapidly running out of questions and conversation and, it seemed, out of luck as well. She thought of Liam and how determined he'd been that she'd had something to do with the suspicious deaths and how she'd dismissed him out of hand.

'How did you select who to kill?' she asked, stringing out the last inevitable moments. 'I mean…there was any number of people you could have chosen, why the ones you did?'

'I wanted to connect you to them. You see, I had to give *you* a motive.'

'Me?'

'Yes.' She smiled another insane smile. 'I was framing you.'

'Oh, God.' Keiva felt her legs go.

'But the detective didn't buy it,' Carol said. 'I could tell that when he interviewed me. That's why I had to wait until he left to finish what I'd planned.'

Keiva allowed herself one painful swallow. 'What had you planned?'

Carol gave her an imperious smirk. 'If it hadn't been for you I would have had Hugh right from the start. You were in the way. I had to make you go away for a very long time.'

'Why didn't you just…kill me instead of all those innocent people?'

'What, and let you get off without suffering? No, I had to make you pay. Everybody thinks you're a wonderful doctor,

I'm sick to death of hearing how talented you are, how you saved lives that others would have lost. My plan was a perfect solution. Your professional reputation would be ruined for all time and no one would ever say how wonderful you are ever again.'

'Carol…' Keiva frantically tried to recall her psych training to negotiate with the disturbed registrar. 'You need help. I should have noticed it earlier, I'm sorry. You're right, I'm not such a great doctor after all, am I?'

'I know what you're doing.' Carol came closer, the point of the syringe dripping as she compressed it. 'But you're not going to talk your way out of this.'

Keiva flattened herself against the wall, preparing herself to fight back, when a voice spoke from behind the registrar.

'Carol, put down the syringe,' Liam said calmly.

The registrar swung around to face him. 'Get out! You're not supposed to be here!'

He stepped towards her slowly, his eyes holding hers. 'Carol…put the syringe on the bedside table. It's over. You have no choice but to back down. There are ten police officers surrounding the premises and five right outside this cubicle. Come on… That's right. Put it down. Good girl. Hugh will be proud of you.'

Keiva watched as Carol did as he said, her thin shoulders slumping in defeat, the sound of her hacking sobs gut-wrenching.

Two policewomen appeared as if by magic and began to escort the distressed registrar away, their soft, placating voices indicating they understood how terribly ill she was.

Liam waited until they'd gone before turning back to where Keiva was pressed up against the wall, her face still white and pinched with the effort of keeping control.

'Hey,' he said softly.

She gave a small tremulous smile, 'Hey, yourself.'

He moved towards her, stopping a mere breath away from

her body. His eyes secured hers as he grazed the soft curve of her cheek with the back of his hand.

'You didn't leave…' she said.

'No.'

She worried her lip for a moment before saying, 'You knew all along, didn't you? You said I was connected in some way.'

'Not as a suspect,' he said. 'I'd figured that out quite early.'

'You didn't say.'

'I had to keep *some* professional boundaries.'

She gave him an ironic look as she stepped away from him. 'How did you come to suspect Carol?' she asked as she absently straightened the covering on Hugh's bed.

'She was edgy on interview and kept dropping little hints about you all the time. She was the only person in this hospital who didn't think you were the best thing that had ever walked in the door. Also, as an anaesthetic registrar, she had unlimited access to drugs. I ran a trace on her and uncovered her childhood history of psychosis. It was covered up by her wealthy parents who hoped her medical training would set her straight.'

She turned back to face him, her expression clouded with guilt. 'I can't help feeling I should have picked up on something before it got to this.'

'You're an A and E doctor, not a psychiatrist. Mental conditions such as Carol Duncan's are not always consistent in how they are manifested. Sufferers can go for months without a psychotic episode, convincing all those around them that they are completely normal.'

'I guess you're right…' She sighed.

'I have some paperwork to do right now. Head Office will need it to process Carol's arrest,' he said. 'After that I was wondering if you'd like to have dinner with me.'

'I don't think that's such a good idea,' she said, without meeting his eyes.

'Why not?'

'You're case file is closed, the investigation is finished and so too is our…association.'

'Is that what you want?' he asked, his tone suddenly brittle. 'For our association, as you call it, to finish?'

She forced herself to meet his penetrating gaze. 'It's what I want.' She held out her hand and gave him an empty smile. 'It was…interesting meeting you, Detective Darcy.'

Liam ignored her hand and, giving her one last angry glance, twitched aside the curtains and left without another word.

'What the hell is going on around here?' Hugh suddenly spoke from the bed behind her.

Keiva rolled her eyes heavenwards and turned to face him.

It was just her luck that the task had fallen to her to tell him what had transpired…

CHAPTER FIFTEEN

KEIVA decided to give her car one last chance.

Three weeks had passed since the incident with Carol Duncan. The press had been and gone and the town was just starting to settle down once more. However, hearing all the details of the disturbed registrar's plan to destroy Keiva's career had taken its emotional toll, and on top of her disappointment over Liam she felt the need to escape for a few days.

She'd had the car serviced the day before and was reasonably confident it would make the distance to the Central Coast where she planned to spend a week lying on the beach to nurse her bruised heart.

She stowed her bag in the boot and got in, unconsciously holding her breath as she turned the key in the ignition.

Nothing.

She took a calming breath and tried again, but apart from a little choking splutter the engine refused to kick over.

'I don't believe this!' she muttered as she got out to lift up the bonnet, kicking the front tyre with her foot on the way past. 'I had you serviced. What more do you want?'

'Keiva Truscott, I have a warrant here for your arrest,' an instantly recognisable voice said from just behind her.

She swung around to see Liam standing with a document in his hand, his eyes shielded by a pair of dark sunglasses.

'Arrest?' She stared at him blankly. 'Whatever for?'

'You're under suspicion of theft,' he said. 'I'm afraid I'm going to have to take you into custody.'

'*Theft?*' Her mouth dropped open.

'That's correct,' he said. 'Grand larceny, to be precise.'

Keiva couldn't believe what she was hearing. 'Is this some sort of joke?'

'I'm afraid not,' he replied solemnly. 'I have it here in black and white.'

'Let me see that!' She snatched it out of his hand before he could stop her and peered down at the typed document.

This is an official warrant for the arrest of Dr Keiva Jayne Truscott who is under suspicion of grand larceny.

She has allegedly stolen the heart of Detective Liam Christopher Darcy who is offering a substantial reward for its immediate return. If she fails to do so, he will have no other choice but to retain her in legal custody until such time as she agrees to marry him.

She looked up at him slowly, the document slipping out of her hand to flutter down to the ground at her feet.

'Well?' he asked, taking off his sunglasses, his grey-blue eyes twinkling. 'Are you going to resist arrest or come quietly?'

She tilted her head at him, a mischievous little smile starting to play about her mouth. 'Are you armed?'

'Armed and dangerous,' he said, giving his back pocket a pat.

'Then I guess I have no other choice.' She stepped closer and held up her wrists. 'Do you want to cuff me?'

'No,' he growled, and hauled her against him. 'I want to kiss you.'

A few breathless minutes later he tipped up her chin to look down into her shining eyes.

'I was so angry when you told me you didn't want to further our relationship. It took me at least two weeks to calm down enough to realise why I was so furious. It wasn't because of my pride. I didn't care a toss for that. What hurt the most was I realised I loved you and wanted to spend the rest of my life with you. I was prepared to do anything to get you to marry me, even if I had to arrest you to do it.'

'I was so afraid you were just using me to fill in the time, she told him. 'I couldn't help falling in love with you but I had no way of knowing if you felt the same.'

'I know.' He gave her a rueful smile. 'My profession has trained me to keep my emotions separate at all times. I didn't even realise what I was feeling until my mother practically hit me over the head with it. She told me to get my butt back out here, and fast—with a proposal you just couldn't refuse.'

'It worked,' she said, linking her arms around his neck. 'But I can't help feeling as if I owe my car an apology. If it hadn't refused to start, I might have left before you got here.'

He gave her a sheepish grin. 'I have a confession to make. I had a word with the mechanic who serviced your car.'

'You did?'

'Sure did. Told him to make sure it got you home and no further. I had some unfinished business with you.'

Keiva's smile threatened to take over her entire face. 'And is your business with me all finished now?' she asked.

'It's just about to begin,' he said, and, scooping her up in his arms, carried her into the house.

1105/059/MB144

Introducing a very special holiday collection

Inside you'll find

Roses for Christmas *by Betty Neels*

Eleanor finds herself working with the forceful Fulk van
Hensum from her childhood – and sees that he hasn't
changed. So why does his engagement to another woman
upset her so much?

Once Burned *by Margaret Way*

Celine Langton ends her relationship with Guy Harcourt
thinking he deserves someone more sophisticated. But why
can't she give back his ring?

A Suitable Husband *by Jessica Steele*

When Jermaine begins working with Lukas Tavinor,
she realises he's the kind of man she's always dreamed of
marrying. Does it matter that her sister feels the same way?

On sale Friday 7th October 2005

MILLS & BOON®

Live the emotion

Her Nine Month Miracle

She's having his baby!

In October 2005, By Request brings back
three favourite romances by bestselling
Mills & Boon authors:

The Pregnancy Discovery
by Barbara Hannay

The Baby Scandal
by Cathy Williams

Emergency Wedding
by Marion Lennox

Pick up these passionate stories.

On sale 7th October 2005

*Available at most branches of WHSmith, Tesco, ASDA,
Borders, Eason, Sainsbury's and most bookshops*

www.millsandboon.co.uk

breast cancer CAMPAIGN

researching the cure

The facts you need to know:

- **One woman in nine** in the United Kingdom will develop breast cancer during her lifetime.

- Each year **40,700** women are newly diagnosed with breast cancer and around **12,800** women will die from the disease. However, survival rates are improving, with on average 77 per cent of women still alive five years later.

- **Men can also suffer from breast cancer**, although currently they make up less than one per cent of all new cases of the disease.

Britain has one of the highest breast cancer death rates in the world. Breast Cancer Campaign wants to understand why and do something about it. Statistics cannot begin to describe the impact that breast cancer has on the lives of those women who are affected by it and on their families and friends.

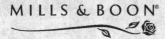

MILLS & BOON®

**During the month of October
Harlequin Mills & Boon will donate
10p from the sale of every
Modern Romance™ series book to
help Breast Cancer Campaign
in *researching the cure*.**

Breast Cancer Campaign's scientific projects
look at improving diagnosis and treatment
of breast cancer, better understanding how
it develops and ultimately either curing the
disease or preventing it.

Do your part to help

Visit <u>www.breastcancercampaign.org</u>

And make a donation today.

researching the cure

FREE!

4 Books
and a surprise gift!

We would like to take this opportunity to thank you for reading this Mills & Boon® book by offering you the chance to take FOUR more specially selected titles from the Medical Romance™ series absolutely FREE! We're also making this offer to introduce you to the benefits of the Reader Service™—

- ★ **FREE home delivery**
- ★ **FREE gifts and competitions**
- ★ **FREE monthly Newsletter**
- ★ **Exclusive Reader Service offers**
- ★ **Books available before they're in the shops**

Accepting these FREE books and gift places you under no obligation to buy, you may cancel at any time, even after receiving your free shipment. Simply complete your details below and return the entire page to the address below. You don't even need a stamp!

YES! Please send me 4 free Medical Romance books and a surprise gift. I understand that unless you hear from me, I will receive 6 superb new titles every month for just £2.75 each, postage and packing free. I am under no obligation to purchase any books and may cancel my subscription at any time. The free books and gift will be mine to keep in any case.

M5ZEF

Ms/Mrs/Miss/Mr ....Initials...
Surname .... **BLOCK CAPITALS PLEASE**
Address...
....
....Postcode ....

Send this whole page to:
UK: FREEPOST CN81, Croydon, CR9 3WZ